Dedalus European Classics
General Editor: Mike Mitchell

Marthe

J.-K. Huysmans

Marthe: The Story of a Whore

Translated with an introduction and notes
by Brendan King

Dedalus

LOTTERY FUNDED

Published in the UK by Dedalus Ltd, Langford Lodge
St Judith's Lane, Sawtry, Cambs, PE28 5XE
email: info@dedalusbooks.com
www.dedalusbooks.com

ISBN 1 903517 47 8
ISBN 978 1 903517 47 5

Dedalus is distributed in the United States by SCB Distributors
15608 South New Century Drive, Gardena, California 90248
email: info@scbdistributors.com   web site: www.scbdistributors.com

Dedalus is distributed in Australia & New Zealand by Peribo Pty Ltd
58 Beaumont Road, Mount Kuring-gai N.S.W. 2080
email: peribo@bigpond.com

Dedalus is distributed in Canada by Disticor Direct-Book Division
695 Westney Road South, Suite 14 Ajax, Ontario, L16 6M9
web site: www.disticordirect.com

Publishing History
First published in Brussels in 1876
First Dedalus edition in 2006
Translation, introduction and notes copyright © Brendan King 2006

The right of Brendan King to be indentified as the translator of this work has been
asserted by him in accordance with the Copyright, Designs and Patent Act, 1988.

Printed in Finland by WS Bookwell
Typeset by RefineCatch Limited, Bungay, Suffolk

A C.I.P. listing for this book is available on request.

THE TRANSLATOR

Brendan King is a freelance writer, reviewer and translator, with a special interest in late nineteenth-century French fiction. He has just completed a PhD on the life and work of the novelist and art critic J.-K. Huysmans.

His previous translations for Dedalus include Huysmans' *Là-Bas* (2001) and *Parisian Sketches* (2004), and in 2006 he revised and annotated the second edition of Robert Baldick's classic biography *The Life of J.-K. Huysmans*.

He lives and works in Paris and on the Isle of Wight.

Plate I: Frontispiece by Jean-Louis Forain for the French
edition of *Marthe, histoire d'une fille*, published by Derveaux in 1879.

INTRODUCTION

Marthe, histoire d'une fille (*Marthe, the story of a whore*) was J.-K. Huysmans' first published novel. Although it has little of the thematic and structural complexity that mark his later novels, notably *A Rebours* (1884), *En Rade* (1887) and *Là-bas* (1891), it nevertheless remains a key text in any analysis of his development as a writer. Moreover, with its Naturalistic handling of emblematic issues such as prostitution, and its lively evocation of low-life Paris with its seedy theatres and even seedier actors, the novel provides a fascinating insight into the social attitudes and conventions of late nineteenth-century France.

When Huysmans began writing the novel in late 1875 or early 1876, he was an aspiring young writer on the fringes of the literary world. His first book, a collection of prose poems entitled *Le Drageoir à épices* (*The Spice Box*), had been published at his own expense in 1874 in an edition of just 300 copies. Although it had sold poorly – only four copies in the first month according to Huysmans himself – it had nevertheless attracted the attention of a handful of critics and influential writers of the period, including Arsène Houssaye and Théodore de Banville, the latter describing the book as 'a jewel cut with the light but firm hand of a master goldsmith' (*Le National*, 18 January 1875). On the strength of this debut work, Huysmans had begun to contribute articles and short sketches to papers such as *Le Musée des*

Deux-Mondes and *La République des Lettres*, and to forge links with other writers and artists both in Paris and in Brussels.

Marthe was not Huysmans' first attempt at writing a novel. Sometime in late 1874 he had conceived the idea of writing an epic novel about the Siege of Paris (1870–71) which would draw on the experiences of his mistress, Anna Meunier, during that traumatic period in the capital's history. Huysmans himself hadn't witnessed the *Siege* at first hand – as a government employee he had been moved to Versailles for the duration – but he had been greatly affected by his first visit to Paris after the hostilities had ended and seen the devastation that had been inflicted on the city he loved. Provisionally entitled *La Faim* (*The Hunger*), the novel had stalled at the first chapter and been banished to a drawer in his desk. Although he would periodically take it out and work on it over the course of the next ten years, it was never completed, and he burned the manuscript a few months before he died.

The impetus for *Marthe* came in the autumn of 1875. At one of his Wednesday night get-togethers with other literary hopefuls such as Ludovic Francmesnil, Gabriel Thyébaut and Henry Céard, Huysmans amused his friends with anecdotes about his tragi-comic liaison with a Bobino soubrette, and his undistinguished adventures in the Garde Nationale during the Franco-Prussian war. Céard, who thought Huysmans should write fiction rather than the prose-poems he seemed so obsessed with, told him he should use the stories as material for a novel.

Huysmans took his advice and picked up his memoir of the Franco-Prussian war, *Le Chant du départ*, which he hadn't touched for three years, and rewrote it as a novella, *Sac au dos* (*Backpack*). Then he embarked on a fictionalised account of his first love affair, in which he reworked his own experiences of brothels, theatres and journalism, as well as utilising Naturalistic documentary techniques in his account of the manufacturing process for artificial pearls and his description of an autopsy room.

Given the close parallels that would later be drawn between his fiction and the events of his life, *Marthe* is significant as the first instance of Huysmans fictionalising his own experience in novel form. This is not to say that *Marthe* is a straightforwardly autobiographical book, or that all the incidents in it have a correlation with the events of Huysmans' actual life. Although it became a commonplace of Huysmans criticism to see all his central characters as thinly disguised portraits of himself, the relationship between autobiography and fiction in his work is never a simple one. It is true there are many parallels between Léo's life and that of the author – his relationship with a Bobino soubrette, his journalistic work for *The Monthly Review*, and so on – but it is nevertheless a mistake to read back from the work into the life. If the episode in which Marthe's lover watches their new-born daughter die is based on personal experience, Huysmans never mentioned it elsewhere, either in his correspondance or in his conversation with friends.

Following the death of his mother on 4 May 1876,

Huysmans was granted a long leave of absence from the Ministry of the Interior, where he had worked since the age of eighteen, and he took the opportunity to concentrate on his writing. By July his novel was progressing well. Convinced that his was the first novel about the life of a prostitute in a licensed brothel, Huysmans was understandably irritated when he read in a newspaper that Edmond de Goncourt was writing a novel on a similar theme and with a similar title, *Le Fille Élisa*. Even worse was the news that it was due for publication in November of that year. Fearing that he would be accused of plagiarism if his novel appeared after Goncourt's, Huysmans extended his leave from the Ministry and at the start of August went to Brussels to arrange the book's publication. In the preface he added to the French edition of *Marthe* of 1879, Huysmans wrote that he had already finished the book when he learned of Goncourt's plans. However, the date and place of composition given at the end of the first edition – 'Brussels August 1876' – seems to infer that the book was still unfinished when Huysmans left Paris to search for a publisher, something which might explain the novel's brevity and its somewhat hurried ending.

Huysmans' decision to look for a publisher in Brussels was not simply a matter of contacts – his friend and fellow contributor to *Le Musée des Deux Mondes*, Camille Lemonnier, had suggested Callewaert as printer and Jean Gay as publisher. Nor was it entirely one of cost, for like *Le Drageoir*, *Marthe* was published at its author's expense and printing was cheaper in Brussels than in Paris. Rather, it was one of political expediency. An insecure French government had begun clamping down on what it saw as threats to the moral health of the nation. In July, the poet Jean Richepin had been fined and sentenced to a month in prison for publishing a collection of poems, *Chanson des gueux* (*Ballad of the Down-and-outs*), one of which, 'Fils de Fille' ('Son of a whore'), had been singled out for particular condemnation by the prosecuting magistrate. Huysmans, who had bought Richepin's book and greatly admired it, feared a similar fate for himself if his novel was published in France and he was keen to avoid the serious consequences this would have had on his job prospects at the Ministry.

The decision to publish in Brussels created more immediate practical problems, and as soon as the book was printed on 12 September 1876, Huysmans set about the difficult task of trying to get copies into France. Somewhat unwisely, he decided to take 400 copies through French Customs himself, with the result that all but a handful were impounded by customs officers.

Although this represented a severe set-back – the total print run would not have exceeded 1,000 and was probably much fewer – Huysmans nevertheless managed to keep hold of a few copies, one of which he sent to Edmond de Goncourt in order to establish his prior claim to the theme of the novel. Somewhat disingenuously, given that he had known about Goncourt's proposed novel since June or July, Huysmans included the following covering letter:

[1 October 1876]

Monsieur,

I have just learned that you are working on a novel called *La Fille Élisa*.

By an unfortunate coincidence I myself have been working for the past year on a book whose subject matter is, it would seem, the same as yours.

This volume, *Marthe*, has just been published in Brussels. It was immediately confiscated in France as an outrage on public morals.

I don't understand it. I had thought in my soul and in my conscience, that I was writing a moral, anti-erotic work of art. Be that as it may, I thought this unfortunate episode might be of interest to you. When I asked the censor to give up the impounded books, he replied: 'It is useless, the subject itself is sufficient to justify their seizure . . .'

The news came as something as a shock to Goncourt – and not just because of the fact that he, one of the fathers of the modern French novel, was being pipped to the post by an obscure newcomer. As the entry in Goncourt's *Journal* shows, the news that Huysmans' novel had attracted the attention of the authorities raised fears and anxieties in his own mind about what might happen to him as the author of an equally scandalously titled novel:

3 October 1876

Yesterday I received a book by M. Huysmans,

Histoire d'une Fille, with a letter which told me the book had been impounded by the censors. That evening, in the back room at the Princess' salon, I talked for a good hour with Doumerc the lawyer about a dispute with my honest solicitor.

From that persecution of a book so similar to my own, and that séance with a man of law, clean-shaven and dressed in black, it came about that night that I dreamt I was in prison, a prison of big stone blocks, like the Bastille in the stage set at the Ambigu theatre. And the curious thing was this: I was imprisoned simply for writing the book *La Fille Élisa*, and that without it having been published, without it even having progressed any further than it is now . . . And I had a vague uneasy feeling, deep down inside me, that the censor had taken advantage of my absence to destroy my manuscript . . .

When Goncourt eventually replied to Huysmans, nearly a month later, his courteous letter betrayed little of his initial state of agitation:

27 October 1876
Monsieur and dear colleague,
I read your captivating book like a presiding judge and I wish the devil himself would carry me off if I could find the least thing in it which could provoke the persecution which this unfortunate, pretty little novel has been the object . . .

I have also read your book, Monsieur, as a novelist, and I compliment you on the rare stylistic and descriptive qualities that shine out, on the vibrant tableaux that jump out from every page in front of one's eyes, and on the delicate *whore-ish* psychology which runs through the whole volume. The only criticism that I will allow myself to make, and you yourself when you are older will recognise the justice of it, is that, young man that you are, you sometimes cannot resist the temptation of an over-literary expression, the charm of a brilliant, showy or curiously archaic word, and this leads you to kill the reality of a well-formed scene, very skilfully, with a literary pistol shot . . .

But once again, my compliments for all the excellent things in your study, and receive Monsieur and dear colleague this expression of my very warm literary sympathy,

Edmond de Goncourt.

This letter marked the start of a regular, if not particularly intimate, correspondence between the two writers which lasted until the older man's death in 1896. Goncourt later invited Huysmans to his *grenier* in Auteuil – one of the most prestigious and influential literary salons of the period – and appreciated the younger man enough to appoint him as one of the ten members of his proposed Académie Goncourt, a literary cenacle set up with the dual purpose of perpetuating his name (and that of his brother) after his death, and encouraging new and imaginative fiction. In the event, by the time the Académie was legally constituted in 1903, Huysmans was the oldest member and became, *ipso facto*, its first President.

If *Marthe* served as a letter of recommendation to one of the leading writers of the previous generation, it was both a calling card for, and a passport into, the circle of writers of his own generation who were beginning to make a name for themselves. Sometime in the autumn of 1876, Henry Céard, who had already taken the plunge and visited Zola in person a few months before, took Huysmans – armed with complimentary copies of both *Le Drageoir* and *Marthe* – to meet the man whom he would come to address in his letters over the next few years as *cher maître*. The visit prompted the following letter in response:

13 December 1876

Monsieur and dear colleague,

I offer my warmest compliments on the novel which you kindly delivered to me. It contains some superb pages. Above all, I like certain bits of description, Marthe and Léo's life as a couple, the dairy, the wineseller's, and in particular Marthe's memories of the whore's life she has led.

But if you would like my honest opinion, I think that the book would benefit from being written with a lighter tone. Your style is rich enough not to abuse it. I am of the opinion that intensity cannot be achieved through the colour

17

of words but through their value. We see everything too blackly, too over-done.

No matter, I've been more than happy to
read your book, because you are surely one of
the novelists of tomorrow. Amid the dearth of
talent there is now, debutants such as yourself
should be welcomed with enthusiasm,

Émile Zola

This auspicious beginning was followed by further
visits to the Zolas, and through them Huysmans and
Céard made the acquaintance of Guy de Maupassant, Paul Alexis and Léon Hennique. Over the
course of the following year or so they met regularly
every Thursday at Zola's house in the Rue Saint-
Georges, and then later at his country retreat at
Médan, in order to discuss their various work pro-
jects. In 1880, all six writers contributed to the anti-
war collection of short stories put together under
Zola's aegis, *Les Soirées de Médan* (*Evenings at
Médan*), which alongside Zola's own *L'attaque du
moulin* (*The Attack on the Mill*), included Huysmans'
Sac au dos, and the story that made the young Guy
de Maupassant's name, *Boule de Suif* (*Blubber-ball*).

Relations between Huysmans and Zola were
cemented in early 1877, when Huysmans was com-
missioned by the Belgian review *L'Actualité* to write
a lengthy study of the older writer and his work. The
result, *Émile Zola et L'Assommoir*, was published in
four parts and artfully combined a profile of the
author with a literary manifesto. Aside from its
fascinating portrait of Zola at home in his study

and its lively defence of his work, *Émile Zola et L'Assommoir* is noteworthy for the discrepancies it reveals between Huysmans' view of Naturalism and that of the movement's figurehead. For despite the fact that Huysmans was often typecast by his critics as one of Zola's 'disciples', there were considerable differences between the two men.

Naturalism can be broadly described as a literary technique that relied on a close, almost scientific documentation of contemporary reality, coupled with a resolute refusal to see the world through the distorting lens of Romantic idealism. As Huysmans put it in *Émile Zola et L'Assommoir*:

Green pustules or rosy flesh, it makes little difference to us; we touch them both, because they both exist, because the lout merits study just as much as the most perfect of men, because fallen women swarm in our cities and have a right there just as much as honest women. Society has two faces: we show them both . . .

Where the two men diverged was not so much in the theory or the technique of Naturalism, but in its application. While Zola used Naturalism as a political tool with which to offer a critique of contemporary society, Huysmans saw it as a means to an aesthetic end. Although Huysmans was generally enthusiastic about Zola's work, he passed over his sociological pretensions in almost dismissive fashion:

It goes without saying that I'm not going to bother myself here with the scientific theory developed by the author, nor with the political questions that everyone thinks so necessary to raise in relation to his books. All *that* interests me, in truth, very little.

This difference in approach can be seen in a comparison with Zola's own 'prostitute' novel, *Nana* (1880), which uses the eponymous prostitute as a means of exposing the hypocrisy and corruption of Second Empire society. By contrast, Huysmans' novel seems less interested in political consciousness-raising than in unpicking what Huysmans' biographer Robert Baldick calls the 'fabric of romantic illusion woven by such writers as Henri Murger'.

But even when he had formally split with Zola, renouncing Naturalism for what he came to see as its gross materialism and its over-simplified reductionism, Huysmans still utilised it as a literary technique. In his later work, he simply expanded its scope to include the transcendental or spiritual aspects of life he felt that Naturalism had overlooked, and in the 1890s he formulated a new aesthetic theory which he referred to in *Là-bas* as 'Spiritual Naturalism'.

Despite their later estrangement, Huysmans' close contact with Zola during the late 1870s benefitted his early career enormously. It helped establish him in the Parisian literary scene, much though he came to detest it, and it was through Zola – and no doubt with his recommendation – that Huysmans switched publisher, his next novel, *Les Sœurs Vatard* (*The*

Vatard Sisters), appearing in the trademark yellow jacket of Zola's publisher, Georges Charpentier. But even with Zola's support and encouragement, Huysmans was still a long way from achieving the respect and celebrity among his peers that *A Rebours* would later earn him, and even further from the volume sales of *Là-bas* (1891), *En Route* (1895) and *La Cathédrale* (1898), which for the first time in his career as a writer gave him the financial security to give up his day job (ironically in the same year he had planned to retire in any case).

In 1876 Huysmans' name was still unfamiliar to the general public; press response to *Marthe* was very limited and what there was was generally hostile. In one of the few reviews of the first edition, for example, Edgard Mey in the Brussels paper, *L'Artiste*, complained about the 'vaguely depressing and sickening feeling' given off by the book's subject matter, and asked: 'What good does it do us to witness the blossoming of this venereal flower?' Almost no Parisian paper mentioned the 1876 edition, though on 15 December 1876, the *Gazette Anecdotique* posted the following unsigned notice:

A strange and very curious little volume has fallen into our hands, printed and published in Brussels a few days since, and which the French censors have forbidden entry into Paris. It is therefore simply out of curiosity that we draw our readers' attention to it. This little book has for title *Marthe, the story of a whore*, and for author Monsieur J.-K. Huysmans, whose first published volume, *The Spice Box*, was sufficiently 'spicy', the title being in no way misleading.

Talent M. Huysmans certainly has, a lot even, but it is a talent misused. He is a realist of the school of Émile Zola, who is a master of the genre, but a master from whom one regrets to see any pupils. The banned book by M. Huysmans cannot be described. It is the story of a whore, and that's all. And M. Huysmans takes us to such places and into such company – and ultimately into such stews of infamy that the reader, however little a prude he might think himself, cannot follow. With this result for the author: that the book sells very expensively under the counter, but the larger public will continue to be ignorant of the name of M. Huysmans until the day he decides to give us, with the real talent that he possesses, a volume that everyone can read.

This kind of hostility to Huysmans' work persisted for a number of years. In a review of *Les Sœurs Vatard*, for example, Firmin Boisson noted simply that *Marthe*, 'the first novel by this shameless novelist, is the brutal and cynical story of a prostitute. It would show a lack of respect to our readers to analyse this obscene production'.

By 1879, the government had relaxed its strictures on censorship and Huysmans decided to publish a French edition. But if he had been unlucky with his first attempt at publishing *Marthe*, his second attempt fared little better, despite the added attraction of a frontispiece engraved by Jean-Louis Forain. The modest publicity campaign planned by the publisher, Derveaux, had to be postponed as it would have been overshadowed by the much larger campaign designed to advertise the publication of Zola's *Nana*. As he walked through Paris, Huysmans must have found it particularly galling to see the huge billboards everywhere advertising Zola's work while his own book was ignored and overlooked.

Huysmans remained proud of the fact that 'his novel about a prostitute in a licensed brothel was the first of its time', as he put it in his pseudonymous autobiographical sketch for *Les Hommes d'aujourd-'hui* (*The Men of Today*) in 1885. Even if it had neither the critical nor the popular success of its close rivals, Goncourt's *La Fille Élisa* (1877) and Zola's *Nana* (1880), *Marthe* was an important milestone in his career as a writer: it placed him solidly in the ranks of the Naturalist movement and it gave him the confidence and the credibility to pursue further explorations in the novel form. For all its faults – its brevity, its uneven narrative line and its uncertain characterisation – the novel contains some well-executed set pieces and shows off Huysmans' acute visual sense and his unerring eye for the strange and the bizarre nestling among the prosaic bric-a-brac of everyday life. If Huysmans' use of language is idiosyncractic and sometimes wilfully perverse, it is nonetheless a perfect vehicle to convey his pessimistic, but grimly humourous vision of an imperfect world and its equally imperfect inhabitants.

NOTE ON THE TRANSLATION

As with most of Huysmans' novels even the title of *Marthe, histoire d'une fille* poses its own problems. In French the word 'fille' can mean 'daughter', 'young girl' or 'prostitute', depending on the context, something which speaks volumes about nineteenth-century values and social relations. I have chosen to translate 'fille' as 'whore' in this instance partly for want of a better English alternative and partly to suggest the element of shock that the original title would have conveyed to its original readership. Huysmans is a difficult writer to render faithfully in English: his novels, especially early works like *Marthe*, are littered with obscure words, archaisms, slang, and neologisms. It would be impossible to provide footnotes for every uncommon usage or for every word belonging to a specialised vocabulary, however I have included notes at the end of the book designed to elucidate references in the text that might otherwise be unclear to the general reader. To avoid distracting the reader with obtrusive footnotes, these have been placed at the back of the book and arranged by chapter and page number.

AUTHOR'S PREFACE TO THE
FRENCH EDITION, 1879

'Printed in Brussels for Jean Gay, publisher, the twelfth day of September 1876, by Felix Callewaert, *père*, printer.'

This book was put on sale on 1st October 1876, in Brussels. Towards the middle of the month of August of the same year I found myself in that city, in the course of overseeing the printing of *Marthe*, when I learned that Monsieur de Goncourt proposed to bring out a novel, *La Fille Elisa*, whose subject matter seemed to resemble that of my own. I should add that the announcement of the book's appearance for 1st November 1876 was incorrect, since *La Fille Elisa* wasn't put on sale in Paris until 20th March 1877.

Be that as it may, I was afraid of being beaten and I speeded up the printing of *Marthe*, and inscribed on its final page the birth certificate reproduced above.

This volume, the first novel I have written, was sold out in a few days. The elevated price which it quickly attained limited the sale to a few amateur collectors of rare books. Monsieur Derveaux felt that people whose interest had been roused by *Les Sœurs Vatard* would perhaps be pleased to be able to obtain more easily this naturalist novel by the same author. Such is the motive that has governed this French edition of *Marthe*.

I had, I admit it, the intention of rewriting it from start to finish, for it seems that I now write in an easier, less tormented style, but on reflection I wanted it to remain as it was, that it preserve all the faults and audacities of youth. Above all, I didn't want anyone to accuse me of having changed a word since the subsequent publication of Monsieur de Goncourt's novel.

I think it useless to argue now about the subject matter I have treated here. The clamorous indignation of the remaining few idealists at the appearance of *Marthe* and *Les Sœurs Vatard* has had little effect on me.

I write what I see, what I feel and what I have lived, writing the best that I can, and that is all.

This explanation is not an excuse, it is simply the statement of the goal I pursue in art.

CHAPTER I

'Look you see, my dear,' Ginginet was saying as he
lolled on the piss-coloured velvet of the sofa, 'you
don't sing too badly, you've a good figure, and
you've a certain feeling for the stage, but that's still
not enough. Take it from me – and it's an old ham
who's tarted himself around the provinces and
abroad telling you this, an old stage-hound as steady
on the boards as a sailor on the sea – well, the thing
is . . . you're still not sexy enough. It'll come, dearie,
but at the moment that wiggle of the hips that
spices up the 'boom' of the bass drum should be
more sensuous. Look here, see . . . I've got legs bowed
like bent fire-tongs, arms as gnarled as vine stalks,
and when I open my mouth I look like the metal frog
on a game of *tonneau*, but I score a thousand points
even with these lead quoits. Pow! The cymbal
crashes, I give it the works, I rasp out the final word
of the chorus, I make the most of a dodgy vocal
flourish, and I've got the public in the palm of my
hand. That's all it takes. Come on, this chorus of
yours . . . spit it out and I'll point out as you sing
where you need a bit of emphasis. One, two, three
and action . . . papa's pinning back his lug-holes,
papa's listening . . .'

'Look, Miss Marthe, here's a letter the girl in the
box-office told me to give you,' mumbled a fat,
snotty-nosed girl.

'Oh, that's really nice, that is!' the girl exclaimed.

'Look, Ginginet, look what I've just got, that's not good manners, is it?'

The actor unfolded the paper and the corners of his mouth curled up almost to his nostrils, revealing his rouge-stained gums and cracking the mask of paint and plaster that covered his face.

'It's in verse!' he cried, visibly alarmed. 'In other words, the man who sent you this hasn't a *sou*. A real gentleman would never send verse!'

The rest of the troupe had crowded round during this exchange. There was an ice-cold wind blowing this evening, and the drafty wings backstage were glacial; all the actors huddled in front of a coal fire blazing in the fireplace.

'What's it say, then?' said an actress in an impudently low-cut dress.

'Hear ye, hear ye,' said Ginginet; and he read, in the midst of rapt attention, the following sonnet:

'To a Singer.
A piccolo that drily squawks and squeaks,
An adenoidal bassoon, an old codger puffing
Fit to spit his fillings down the neck of his trombone,
A violin buzzing like an old rebeck,

A wheezing flageolet to whose beak one gives suck
A grouchy cornet, a bass drum that booms;
This, with its conductor as fat as a barrel,
Scrofulous, and ugly enough to hold in check

Even the most amorously inclined of women,

Is the theatre orchestra. – And yet it's here,
That you, my only love, you, my only delight,

You croon those vulgar refrains every night,
And, your heart in your mouth, eyes closed,
   arms open wide,
You smile at the rabble, O Queen of the fair!'

And it wasn't even signed.

'I say, Ginginet, that's what you call sticking it to our conductor; you should show him this doggerel – that'd cut him down to size, the old scraper!'

'Come on ladies, on stage now,' shouted a man in a black hat and a blue Macfarlane coat; 'to your places, the orchestra's just striking up!'

The women got up, threw shawls over their bare shoulders, shaking and shivering, and, followed by the men who abandoned their pipes and their games of bezique, they all filed out through the little door that led to the wings.

The duty fireman was at his post and despite being half-dead with the cold his eyes burned as he stared at the under-petticoats of some of the dancers who had strayed into this revue. The stage-manager knocked three times, and the curtain slowly went up, revealing a packed house.

Without a doubt, the most interesting spectacle was not what was happening on stage, but in the audi-torium. The Bobino theatre, known as the 'Bobinche', wasn't, like those of Montparnasse, Grenelle and the other old suburbs of Paris, full of working men who wanted to listen seriously to some dramatic work. The Bobino's clientele was students and artists, a boisterous and cynical race if ever there was one. They didn't come to this miserable shed lined with hideous purple wallpaper to swoon in front of leaden melodramas or madcap comedies; they came to shout, to laugh, to interrupt the performance – in short, to have a good time. The curtain had scarcely risen before the braying began; but Ginginet was not a man to be worried by a little thing like that, his long dramatic career had accustomed him to hisses and catcalls. He waved graciously to those who were interrupting him, chatted with them, sprinkled his lines with jokes aimed at the troublemakers, and soon had the whole audience applauding him. The show, on the other hand, went pretty badly, and was barely limping along by the second scene. The audience started to get restless again. What it appreciated above all was the entrance of an enormous actress whose nose seemed to be marinading in a lake of fat. The tirade of verse that spouted from the bunghole of this human wine-barrel was punctuated by a great battery of drumming from the stalls and the poor woman was so bewildered she didn't know whether to stay or make a run for it. Then Marthe appeared: the din ceased.

She looked ravishing in her costume, which she had cut out of moire and silk remnants herself. A pink corselet decorated with fake pearls, an exquisite pink corselet of that faded, almost lifeless pink you find in Levantine fabric hugged her hips, which were barely contained within their prison of silk; and with her helmet of magnificent red hair, her provocative lips, moist, hungry and red, she was enchanting, irresistibly seductive.

The two most fearless hawkers, who had been answering one another from orchestra pit to gallery, ceased their shouts of 'Key rings! Keep your keys safe! Five *centimes*!' and 'Lemonade, beer, orgeat, a *sou*!' Supported by the prompter and by Ginginet, Marthe was applauded extravagantly. As soon as her song was over the row started up again even more furiously. A painter sitting in the stalls and a student in a red waistcoat perched up in the gods set to with even greater gusto, catcalling and heckling to the immense delight of the audience who were bored to tears by the show.

Leaning against one of the flats by the side of the footlights, Marthe was looking into the hall and asking herself which of these young men could have written her the letter, but every eye in the house was fixed on her, and all were inflamed at the sight of her bosom; it was impossible for her to discover among all these admirers the one who had sent her the sonnet.

The curtain fell without her curiosity being satisfied.

The following evening, the actors were in a foul mood, they expected another riot and the director, who, due to a shortage of funds also fulfilled the functions of stage manager, was feverishly pacing up and down the stage, waiting for the curtain to rise.

He suddenly felt a tap on his shoulder and, turning around, found himself face to face with a young man who shook him by the hand and very calmly asked him:

'You still keeping well, then?'

'But . . . but yes, not bad . . . and you?'

'Oh, I get by, thank you very much. Now, let's understand each other: you don't know me, and I don't know you. Well, I'm a journalist and I intend to write a marvellous article on your theatre.'

'Oh! Pleased to meet you, really delighted, absolutely! But what paper do you write for?'

'*The Monthly Review.*'

'Don't know it. And when does it come out?'

'Generally every month.'

'I see . . . well take a seat.'

'Thank you, but I won't take you up on that just now.'

And he rushed off to the green-room, where the actors and actresses were gossiping.

He was a canny man, this newcomer. He had a friendly word for an actor here, a kind word for an actress there, promising a good write-up for each of them, above all for Marthe, who he stared at with such a greedy eye it wasn't difficult for her to guess that he was the author of her letter.

He returned in the days that followed and paid court to her; to be brief, he succeeded one evening in dragging her home with him.

Ginginet, who was watching the young man's little game, fell into a furious rage which he unleashed in great torrents on the head of Bourdeau, his colleague and friend.

The two of them were seated in a bar of the lowest kind to drink a glass or three together. In truth, I have to say that Ginginet had been painting the town the most liveliest of reds since the afternoon – he claimed to have sand dunes in his throat that he was irrigating with great waves of wine. Soon he began to nod, his head nodding on to the table, his nose dipping in his glass and, without looking at his companion who was dozing, more drunk even than he was himself perhaps, he belched out a monologue stippled and cross-hatched by a series of jerks and hiccoughs.

'Stupid, that girl, very stupid, sublimely stupid, oh yes. To take a lover's all very well if he's rich; but if not, better to stick with Ginginet's ugly mug – not handsome, that's true – Ginginet, or young, that's true as well, but he's an artist! an artist! but she prefers this fancy-boy who writes verse! a profession for wasters, that's as clear as my voice – not this evening though, I'm slurring like anything, which reminds me of a song I used to sing at Amboise when I was the lead tenor at the Grand Theatre – what a glorious past, eh – a song called 'My wife and my umbrella.' They weren't so stupid, were they, those couplets! Sure a woman and a brolly, aren't they the same thing? They both turn on you and let you down in bad weather! Hey, Bourdeau, are you listening? I was just saying I've been like a father to her, a noble father who lets her flutter her eyes at all those rich young men, but in front of paupers, in front of down-and-outs like him, a good-for-nothing! *zut alors*! then I become the serious father,' and, moved

35

to tears, Ginginet accentuated his soliloquy with a vigorous blow of his fist on the table, sloshing the wine in his glass and splashing his old bald pate with big red drops.

'It's raining outside, it's raining inside,' he muttered, 'goodnight all, I'm going to bed. Hey, Bourdeau, hey! sleepyhead, raise yourself, it's your old mucker calling! The one who used to sing I-don't-know-how-many songs at Amboise ... Ah! God's blood, what lungs, what a voice I used to have! Oh misfortune of misfortunes, to think it all went at the same time as my hair! Hey, you, jack-the-lad,' he shouted at the waiter, 'these coins are burning a hole in my pocket so put 'em out, there are five pints to pay for; and now, onward, ye knights! And as for the bourgeoisie, to hell with 'em!'

And so saying he grabbed Bourdeau, who was dragging his heels behind him, by the left arm, and, whistling through his nose, puffing out his belly and waddling like a bear, he sang at the top of his voice a eulogy in honour of fine wine and not-so-fine women.

CHAPTER II

After ten years of fruitless struggle and impatiently endured poverty, Sébastien Landousé, artist, got married, just as he was starting to make a name for himself, to Florence Herbier, worker in artificial pearls. Unfortunately his health, already under-mined by love-making and over-work, declined day by day, so much so that after a chest infection that laid him low in his bed for six long months he died and was buried, for want of money, in a forgotten corner of a communal grave.

Apathetic and lethargic by temperament, his wife bucked up under the blow that had struck her and put herself valiantly to work, but after her daughter, Marthe, had reached her fifteenth year and finished her apprenticeship, she died in her turn, and, like her husband, was buried in some cemetery somewhere.

Soon Marthe, as a worker in artificial pearls, was earning four francs a day, but the job was so exhaust-ing and unhealthy she often wasn't up to it.

Artificial pearls are made from the scales of a fish, the bleak, which are ground down and reduced to a kind of porridge that the worker has to keep stirring. In the slightest heat this mixture of water, ammonia and fish-scales spoils and becomes a sink of infection, so you have prepare the paste in a cool cellar. The older it is, the more valuable it becomes. It is pre-served in carefully-sealed bottles, and from time to time the diluted ammonia solution is renewed.

As with certain wine merchants, these bottles bear the details of the year they were filled, and just like the 'pure septembral juice' this gleaming mash improves with age. Anyway, even without labels, one would still have recognised the young bottles from the old, the former having a dark grey tarnish, while the latter seem to gleam like quicksilver. Once the mixture is sufficiently thick and consistent, the worker has to blow it, using a blowpipe, into a spherical or ovoid glass bead – ball- or pear-shaped according to the required shape of the pearl – and then wash it with ethanol, which is also blown through a pipe. This latter operation is intended to dry the glaze; all that remains after that, to give the pearls weight and preserve their silvery lustre, is to drip virgin wax inside. If it has a proper silver-grey 'orient', if it's what the manufacturer calls a *demi-fin*, it'll be worth anything from 3 francs to 3 fr 50.

In this fashion Marthe spent her days filling tiny beads, and in the evening when her work was done she would go to Montrouge to see her mother's brother, a violin-maker, or else go back to her own lodgings where, frozen by the cold in the empty apartment, she would hurry to bed in order to drown the melancholy of those long light evenings in sleep.

She was, moreover, a peculiar girl. Strange enthusiasms, a disgust for her job, a hatred of poverty, an unhealthy longing for the unknown, a despair that had nothing of resignation about it, poignant memories of the wretched, hunger-filled days spent with her sick father; a conviction, born of the spurned artist's bitterness, that security acquired at the cost of all manner of cowardice and corruption is all that can be expected here below; a craving for luxury and glamour, a morbid languor, a neurotic disposition which she inherited from her father and a certain innate laziness she got from her mother who had been so courageous in adversity and so feckless when necessity no longer goaded her on – all this seethed and boiled furiously within her.

Unfortunately the workshop was not the place to bolster her faltering courage or lend support to her hard-pressed virtue.

A workshop full of women is the antechamber of the VD clinic. It wasn't long before Marthe was hardened to the conversations of her workmates; bent over their bowls of fishscales all day, in between blowing a couple of pearls, they would gossip away endlessly. In truth, their conversation varied little: it always turned on the subject of men. One girl was living with a well-off gentleman – got so much a month from him – and they all admired her new lockets, her rings and her ear-rings; all were jealous of her and pressed their lovers to give them similar trinkets. A girl is lost once she starts mixing with other girls: the conversation of schoolboys is as nothing compared to that of working girls; a workshop is a touchstone for virtue, you rarely come across gold there, but brass abounds. A young girl doesn't 'fall', as the novelists put it, from love or being carried away by her senses, but mostly from vanity – and a little bit of curiosity. Marthe used to listen to accounts of her workmates' adventures, their sweet or deadly struggles with the opposite sex, her eyes wide and her mouth dry with excitement. The others laughed at her and called her 'little chickie'. To hear them talk, all men were absolute idiots. One of the girls had made a fool of her man the night before and kept him waiting for an appointment; it only made him all the more hungry for her; another was making her lover's life a misery, but the more unfaithful she was the more he loved her. All of the girls deceived their admirers or twisted them round their little fingers, and all of them gloried in their power. If Marthe blushed now, it wasn't because of the filthy stories she heard, she blushed because she wasn't on a par with her workmates. She was no longer in two minds whether to give herself, she was just waiting for the right occasion.

Besides, the life she was leading was insupportable. Never a laugh, never any fun! The only entertainment she had was provided at her uncle's house, a real dump that was rented by the week and stuffed, in no particular order, with uncle, aunt, children, dogs and cats. In the evenings they played lotto, that sublimely stupid game, marking the scores with trouser buttons; on public holidays they drank a glass of mulled wine between games and sometimes even had peeled roasted chestnuts or boiled sweet chestnuts. These pauper's pleasures exasperated her, and she preferred the company of one of her girl friends, who was living with her man. But they were both young and never left off kissing each other. The situation of a third person in the middle of such couples is always ridiculous; so she would leave them feeling sadder and angrier than before. Oh, she'd had enough of this solitary life, of those eternal torments of Tantalus, of that unappeasable itch for affection and for money. It was necessary to put an end to it, and she daydreamed about it.

Every evening she was followed home by a man of advanced years who promised her the moon; and every evening a young man who lived in the same building on the floor below hers brushed against her on the stairs and quietly begged her pardon when his arm touched hers. Her choice was never in doubt. In the balancing-scales of her heart, the old one carried the day, for where one could only offer his charm and his youth, the other threw in that sword of Brennus: prosperity and wealth. He also had a certain cultured air about him which flattered the young girl, because her companions only had louts, draper's assistants and hardware-store clerks for lovers. She succumbed – without even the excuse of an irresistible passion, the burning fire of which compels one to cry out and abandon oneself body and soul – she succumbed . . . and was overwhelmed with disgust.

The next day, however, she related her lapse, which she now regretted, to her companions. She put on a show of pride about her valiant deed and, in front of the whole workshop, took the arm of the old letch who had bought her. But her courage didn't last long; her nerves couldn't stand the strain; and one night she showed the old man and his money the door, and resolved to take up her former way of life. But it's the same story as with those who take up smoking: at first, sick to the stomach, they swear never to do it again – and then do it again until the stomach consents to be tamed. After one cigarette, another; after the first lover, a second.

This time, she wanted to love a young man, as if that could be arranged to order! The other one loved her . . . sort of, but he was so gentle and so respectful that she couldn't resist making him suffer. They ended up separating by common consent. Then she did as the others did; but after a week, three days, two days or one, she'd be fed up with the importunity of their unwanted caresses. In the meantime she fell ill and, as soon as she recovered, was abandoned by her latest lover; to add to her misfortune, the doctor expressly ordered her to give up her job as a pearl-blower. What was she to do now? What was to become of her? Here was misery, made more oppressive because the memory of the good-fortune she had tasted with her first lover constantly recurred to her. She tried her hand at other jobs, but the poor wages she earned discouraged her from making any further efforts. One fine evening hunger drove her into the venal mire, and there she sprawled, never to get back up.

Then she drifted along with the flow, spending whatever chance earnings she got on food, and enduring fasts whenever times were hard. Her apprenticeship in this new trade was soon complete; she was now a slave to anyone who passed, a hired labourer of the passions. One evening in a dancehall, when she was touting for custom alongside a tall, willowy slut with eyes the colour of sienna, she met a young man who seemed to be looking for adventure. Marthe, with her lips the colour of redcurrant, her endearing pout whenever he teased her, her imposing looks like some suburban goddess and her burning glances, so captivated this young innocent, that she brought him home with her. This chance meeting soon developed into a regular occurrence. They even ended up living together. Chased from hotel to hotel, they eventually snuggled up in a squalid hole in the Rue du Cherche-Midi.

The house had all the charm of a slum. A rusty door streaked blood-red and ochre yellow, a long dark corridor the walls of which oozed black drops like coffee, and a sinister staircase that creaked at every footstep and was impregnated with the foul stench of drains and the smell of the lavatories whose doors swung open in the slightest breeze. It was on the third floor of this house that they chose a room with floral wallpaper, which in places had been scratched off, letting through a fine rain of plaster. There were none of the usual painted alabaster or porcelain vases in these lodgings, none of those clocks without hands or mirrors speckled with fly-shit; they didn't even have that ubiquitous luxury of the furnished room, the colour print of Napoléon wounded in the foot and getting back onto his horse. The bare walls pissed drops of yellow liquid and the tiled floor, with its patches of varnished scarlet, looked like diseased skin, marbled with red eruptions. The only furniture was a dirty wooden bed, a table lacking its drawer, chintz curtains stiff and black with grime, a chair without a bottom and an old armchair which split its sides alone by the fireplace, laughing out of all its crevasses and, as if to taunt them, sticking out tongues of black horsehair through all the splits in its velvety mouths.

They stayed there for eight weeks, living on their wits, drinking and eating indescribable things. Marthe was beginning to long for another way of life when she discovered that she was a few months pregnant. She burst into tears, swore to her lover that the child was not his, said he was free to go – this ruse binding him irredeemably to her – and made the poor wretch agree with her resolve to deprive herself of every luxury in order to put aside the money needed for a midwife.

They could have spared themselves the trouble – she fell downstairs and brought on the birth. On a clear night in December, when neither had a *sou*, she felt the first pangs of labour. The young man rushed out in search of a midwife, whom he brought back with him straightaway.

'But it's freezing in here,' cried this bonnet-wearing angel as she entered the room. 'We must light a fire at once.'

Fearing that if the woman guessed how poor they were she would ask to be paid in advance, Marthe asked her lover to look for the key to the coal-cellar – it should be either in the pocket of her dress or on the mantelpiece. He was so bewildered that he began to look for the key in earnest, when suddenly Marthe stiffened, uttered a long groan and fell back, white and inert, onto the bed. She had just brought a little girl into the world.

The midwife washed the child, wrapped it up and

left, announcing that she would return the following day at dawn.

That night was unbelievably forlorn. The girl groaned and complained that she could not sleep; the boy, dying of cold, sat in the armchair and rocked the poor mite who wailed in a lamentable fashion. Towards three in the morning snow fell and the wind started howling through the passageway, rattling the ill-fitting windows, slapping the candle-flame around which was sputtering madly, and sending ashes from the fireplace flying into the room. The baby was frozen and hungry; to make matters worse its swaddling clothes came undone and, numbed by the blasts which froze his hands, the young man couldn't put them back in place. And to add one last horribly trivial detail, this fireless room made him so ill that he no longer knew what to do, and the poor child cried louder and louder whenever he stopped rocking her.

The consequence of this vigil was that both the child and the man died: the one from weakness and cold, and the other from an abnormal dropsy which this night helped bring on. The girl alone emerged from this torture, more radiant and more alluring than ever. For a while she lived off what she could get hanging around street-corners, until the evening when, discouraged at not finding the morass in which she could earn her bread, she met one of her old pearl-factory workmates. This girl hadn't needed to strike a reef: she'd gone down with all hands on the open seas. This meeting decided Marthe's fate. The other girl flaunted the profits of her state; Marthe drank a couple of glasses too many, accompanied her friend to the entrance of the lair and chanced a foot inside thinking she could take it out whenever she felt like it.

The next day she was a hired servant in a pick-up joint.

CHAPTER III

Although she almost drank herself to death trying to blot out the abominable life she was leading, she couldn't resign herself to the self-abnegation, the unrelenting prison-sentence of this odious trade which makes no allowance for repugnance or fatigue.

Nor could the bleak degradation of those binges blot out that terrible life, which throws you from eight in the evening to three in the morning onto a sofa-bed; which forces you to smile, whether you're happy or sad, ill or not; which forces you to stretch out next to some awful drunk, to submit to him, to satisfy him, a life more terrible than any hell dreamt up by the poets, than any slave galley or any prison ship, because there is no state, however demeaning or miserable it is, that equals in abject labour and in grim weariness the trade of these unfortunates.

On this particular evening Marthe's feelings of anxiety and disgust were especially intense. For the past twenty minutes she had been lying prostrate on a pile of cushions, pretending to listen to the chatter of her companions, trembling at the slightest sound of an approaching footstep.

She felt sick and tired, as if emerging from a lengthy debauch. From time to time the pain seemed to abate and she looked with a dazzled eye at the splendours that surrounded her. Those candle chandeliers, those walls hung with a dull red satin and embossed with white silk flowers gleaming like specks of silver, were dancing in front of her eyes, glittering like white sparks against the crimson of a brazier. Then her vision cleared and she saw herself in a huge Venetian glass mirror, shamelessly sprawled on a banquette, her hair fixed up as if she were going to a ball, bare flesh emphasised by lace underwear that was spiced with a strong perfume.

She couldn't believe this image was herself. She looked in astonishment at her powdered arms, her charcoaled eyebrows, her lips red as bloody meat, her legs sheathed in cherry-coloured silk stockings, her heaving and tremulous breasts, at all the disturbing allure of her flesh which quivered beneath the frills of her dressing-gown. Her eyes frightened her, rimmed with black eye-liner, they seemed to her to be strangely hollowed-out and she discovered in their unexpected depths I don't know what childish and vulgar expression that made her blush beneath her make-up.

Then she stared with stupefaction at the strange postures of her companions, odd-looking, vulgar beauties, provocative sluts, butches and skinny waifs, stretching out on their bellies, their heads in their hands, squatting on stools like dogs or draping themselves like faded finery over the edges of sofas, their hair done up every which way: waved spirals, crimped curls, curly ringlets, gigantic chignons studded with pink and white daisies, fringes of artificial pearls, black or blonde manes, pomaded or dusted with snow-white powder.

Their sleeveless dressing-gowns, fastened at the shoulder by ribbon-like straps of delicate silk, hung loosely, and beneath their diaphanous folds one caught revealing glimpses of the enticing nudity of their bodies.

Jewels glittered, rubies and fake-gems caught passing rays of light, and, standing before a mirror, turning her back to the door, a woman with arms raised drove a hair-pin into the dark mass of her hair. Her long gauze dressing-gown rose with the movement of her arms, leaving a wide space between its pale vapour and the granite of her flesh; her breasts perked up too with the lifting of her elbows and their orbs bulged, white and firm, against the rose-patterned edging of the material. A line running from her slightly tilted neck broke up into the rolling folds of flesh which linked her hips, and, furrowed by a deep curve, the snowy curves of her rump bulged over her legs, which flushed pink above the knee from the grip of her garters.

And this room, completely saturated with the torrid odour of amber and patchouli, was in a complete state of uproar, of chaos and commotion! There were sudden bursts of laughter like rifle-fire, and disputes sprang up in every direction, bearing waves of innuendo and obscenity in their precipitous wake.

Suddenly a bell rang out. Silence fell as if by magic. All the girls sat down, and those who were dozing on the banquettes suddenly sat up and rubbed their eyes, trying to reignite that flame in their glance for a few moments, so that some passing man might walk their plank and board them.

The door opened and two young men came into the room.

The new girl lowered her eyes, hiding as best as she could, trying to make herself as small as possible so as not to be noticed, staring fixedly at the rose-pattern of the carpet, sensing the stare of these two men who undressed her with their eyes.

Oh, how she despised these men who came to see her! She didn't understand that most of them who lingered in her presence came to forget, in the restlessness of her bed, their long-endured frustrations, their bitter resentments, their inexhaustible sufferings; she didn't understand that after having been deceived by the women they loved – after having sipped heady wines from mousseline glasses and lacerating their lips on the broken shards – most of them now wanted to drink nothing but cheap plonk from coarse public-house tankards.

One of the men made her a sign. She didn't move, casting imploring glances at her companions, but they all laughed and made fun of her; the Madame only stared at her with lifeless eyes. Afraid, she got up like a mule which, after having been beaten, dashes off suddenly under the sting of the whip; she crossed the room, stumbling, deafened by a hail of jeers and bursts of laughter.

She went upstairs, supporting herself against the wall, feeling a wave of bitter nausea surge in her stomach; a maid opened the door and stood back to let them pass.

The man went in, and then, almost fainting, she let the heavy curtain fall behind her.

She woke the next morning, hungover with disgust, and with but one aim, one idea in her mind: to escape from this shameful house, to go far away and forget her unforgettable troubles.

The atmosphere of that room, heavy with the musky smell of make-up, its padlocked windows, its thick hangings warmed by a still-glowing fire, and its bed, dishevelled and ransacked by the pillages of the night, disgusted her almost to sickness. Everyone else was asleep; she dressed and hurried down stairs, drew the bolts and darted into the street. Ah, now she could breathe again! She wandered at random, thinking of nothing. She was as if drunk. Suddenly, she was gripped by a sense of her misfortunes, she remembered that she was on the run from debauchery, that she had broken parole, and she looked around her like a frightened animal.

She found herself at the bottom of the Boulevard Saint-Michel just as two policemen were calmly walking down towards the Seine. An indefinable anguish seized her by the throat and her legs buckled; it seemed to her that these men were coming to arrest her and drag her off to the station. The sun, which streamed down in golden drops on to the tree-lined road, appeared to be shining on her alone, revealing to everyone just what she was. She fled down one of the gloomy little streets that linked the Boulevard Saint-Michel to the Place Maubert. She felt more at ease in the shadows of the doorways that gave onto the pavement. She got her breath back in one of those passageways that smells like a dank cellar, and then resumed her walk. During these few minutes rest, her confusion abated, she thought of going to one of her girl friends who lived on the Rue Monge and asking for shelter; she knocked fruitlessly at her door and, assured by the concierge that she would be back soon, took off for a saunter, walking the length and breadth of the street. She stared with a distracted air in the window of a toyshop: marbles, picture books, wooden puppets, small glazed green cooking-pots for children, ribbed perfume bottles with ground stoppers capped with white leather tops, bottles of red ink, packets of sewing needles wrapped in black paper and stamped in gold with the coat of arms of England, religious images and Mengin crayons.

After she had looked at everything in this miserable display without really seeing it, she went back to the concierge. Her friend had still not returned.

She walked off again; a hot thirst was burning in her throat; she stopped in front of a wine-merchant's and debated with herself whether she should go in. She had become more timorous than a child. She remained for a good ten minutes stuck in front of the window display, reading under her breath the labels on the bottles, looking at square flasks of Danzig brandy with their showers of gold, at litres of orgeat like congealed oil, at bottles of cognac and of cassis, and liqueur-jars full of pink cherries, green plums and yellow peaches. Finally, she pushed open the door and the smell of alcohol grabbed her by the throat. She asked the publican for a half-litre of wine and a siphon of soda-water.

It seemed to her that the landlord was staring at her insolently. Had he, too, guessed from what prison

she had escaped? Anxious and ashamed, she took
refuge in a little room adjoining the bar.

The publican made her wait for at least a quarter
of an hour before serving her; then he threw her
drink on the table and hurried off to serve a man
who, on pushing open the door, shouted:

'A shot of juice old chap and a crust of bread!'

'Well, if it isn't Monsieur Ginginet,' the man said.

'Yes, it's me. I've been running around like a grey-
hound since this morning. You see, old chap, I've
been asked by the boss to put a new company
together at the Bobino Theatre. No money, but he
wants stars of the first magnitude – comets, what!
That's his motto that man. Well, I dashed round to
Roland, to Machut, and to Adolphe, and I've hired
'em all; all I'm missing is singers;' and as he spoke,
Ginginet cut off a big hunk of bread and downed
several glassfuls, one after another. In between two
swigs he noticed Marthe, who was sitting, sombre,
almost sullen, at the back of the room. Then he
started to trot out his backstage *bon mots*, to reel off
a string of pleasantries. When he saw her smile, he
invited her to have a coffee with him; she refused, but
this devil of a man was so dapper, so jolly, he had
such a good-old-boy air about him, that she ended up
having a conversation with him. Ginginet examined
her: 'She's superb,' he murmured; 'with a new frock
she'll set the house on fire. She's got a guilty, down-
and-out look about her, she's done something silly,
she probably hasn't even got anywhere to live, if
she's got half a voice I'll engage her straight away; a
moonbeam picked up in a pub! I'll teach her to sing

and act within a fortnight. She may not have any talent, but she's pretty and that's the main thing in the theatre.'

She accepted: she felt as if she'd been saved. A fortnight later, she made her debut at the Bobino.

This new life pleased her. Like all unfortunate women whom poverty and procurement have dragged into the brothels of a town, she experienced, in spite of herself – and in spite of the horrible disgust which had assailed her ever since her first client – that strange feeling of regret, that terrible sickness which makes every woman who has lived this kind of life return and plunge into it again some day or other. That life of passions and drinking-bouts, of broken sleep, of perpetual chatter, of comings and goings, of entrances and exits, of going up and down stairs, of lassitude overcome by alcohol and laughter, exerts a fascination over these poor women like the dizzying allure of the abyss.

What saved Marthe from this appalling relapse was partly the shortness of the time she had stayed in the brothel, but it was chiefly the distractions of backstage life, the exhibition of herself in front of the burning eyes of her audience, the camaraderie of the other actors, the hustle and bustle every minute of the evening while she dressed and rehearsed her part. For her, a passion for the theatre was the strongest possible antidote against the poison she had absorbed.

CHAPTER IV

Making their way arm-in-arm up the road, Marthe and Léo were chatting inanely away to each other. They were going the wrong way up the Rue Madame, heading towards the Croix-Rouge.

The conversation became more and more fatuous. Compliments about her dress, about her voice, the gossip at the theatre, her womanly questions on the subject of the street where he lived – all were exhausted. A dog watched them go by on the pavement and howled for no reason: they talked about dogs. He preferred cats, she, those curly-haired bow-wows, those awful pugs whose breath stinks when they eat meat or anything sweet. This discussion soon came to an end. They didn't say a word for a few minutes, then a drunk staggered out of a side-street, bumping against the walls, and they complained about drunkards, then fell silent. A policeman passed. She felt a slight shiver run down her back. He tried to cheer her up, but she didn't seem to hear him. In truth, it was just as well they had arrived at his place.

The gas-lamp was out. Léo took Marthe's hand and guided her across the courtyard as far as the door to the passage. There, they stopped; he lit a wax taper, and she saw the lower steps of a stairwell that twisted up into the darkness. When he opened his door, a big coal fire was staining the drapes of the little room with slabs of red and illuminating the glass of the picture-frames hanging on the walls with sparkling flames. Marthe took off her hat and her sable wrap and sat down in a huge leather armchair which he rolled closer to the fire. Squatting at her feet, he stared at her, marvelling at her waist, which was suppler than a reed stem, and dying of longing to kiss her hair, which twisted in mad curls over the snowy-pink of her neck. A hairpin had come undone and a long spiral of hair uncoiled on to her dark green, almost black, dress, which encased her like a Japanese kimono, outlining the curves of her breasts and the arc of her hips. With her splendidly radiant black-lashed eyes, her glowing red lips and her rounded cheeks, she looked, minus that sumptuously picturesque costume, like Saskia, Rembrandt's first wife, whose image Ferdinand Bol has conjured up for us in his magnificent portrait.

Marthe got up. 'Look at them,' she said, 'all those people drinking,' and, with a pink almond-shaped nail, she touched a copy of Jordaens' *The Bean King*, then she laughed out loud at the sight of this King wearing a tinsel crown, his hair spilling out every which way over the napkin round his neck. She was amused by this company of revellers singing, smoking and shouting at the top of their voices: 'The King drinks! the King drinks!' Léo had taken her hand and, all the while kissing it, showed her the women in the picture: the pot-bellied slattern wiping her child's backside while a dog sniffs at it, and two others, slim blondes who, seven sheets to the wind, were roaring with laughter and drinking wine the colour of light, and beer the colour of amber.

Marthe had a sudden vision of revelries in times gone by.

But these extravagances, these high spirits, this abundance of flesh *à la* Rubens, these swathes of lily-white and vermilion, this rich profusion, this sumptuosity of fleshliness, these swirls, these waves of carmine and mother of pearl – didn't hold her attention for long. She looked, without pausing, at several other pictures, then stopped thoughtfully in front of an engraving by Hogarth, one of the episodes from *A Harlot's Progress*. Those women in their low dresses, that drunken young man who was being robbed of his watch by a ravishing young thing, those benches littered with overturned glasses, those tarts swearing and spitting and threatening each other with knives, that hussy, her corsets and petticoats lying in a crumpled heap on the floor, pulling her top-boots over her silk stockings, that creature who was pocked with beauty-spots on her lips and forehead, with one breast hanging out of her chemise, and those two ragged pimps at the door hooting like owls and reflecting a candle-flame against a large copper dish – all this evoked in her very precise memories and she remained fascinated, silent . . . and then, as if awaking from a dream, she said quietly to herself: 'Yes, that's just how it is!'

She sat down again in the armchair; as for him, he sat astride a low fireside chair and poked the fire. They were both ill at ease. She was thinking of her former life. All her old memories were reawakening. That atmosphere of the brothel, that hint of the whore she had tried so hard to eradicate, came back all of a sudden and overpoweringly obsessed her. The more she watched herself, the more strange words, inappropriate remarks and expressions that she had wanted to forget returned to her mind and, despite herself, sprang to her lips. She broke off the conversation that Léo had taken up again and stared at the hearth with a look so sombre that her lover didn't know what to say or do.

While all this was going on the clock, which had been chattering away without respite as if to mock their silence, struck two. Martha looked up. Léo took the opportunity to say to her:

'I think it's time we went to bed.'

And as she went into the other room, he curled up in the armchair she had just vacated and immersed himself in his thoughts.

Truth to tell, they were far from happy. This boy had early on thrown off the yoke of maternal discipline and he had so misused his newly-acquired freedom that debauchery, morality's avenging angel, had branded him body and soul. Conscious of a real talent that any artist would have respected – and any bourgeois would have scorned – he had thrown himself head first into the quagmire of the world of letters. Unfortunately there was only a foot of water at the point he dived in; he bruised himself so badly on the stones at the bottom that he came up discouraged before he'd even tried to get to open sea. He lived by his pen, which is as much to say he starved, and as a result of over-elaborating his thoughts, of trying to express the strange ideas that haunted him, he

strained his nerves and an immense fatigue overwhelmed him. From time to time, on good days, he
would write a page or two swarming with terrible
grotesques, with succubi or phantoms like those in
Goya's pictures, but the next day he found himself
incapable of throwing four lines together, and would
thrash out, after the most incredible effort, vague
characters who defied analysis and who were beyond
the grasp of any critic.

What he dreamed of as a mental stimulant, as an
alarm bell that would awaken his drowsing talent,
was that monstrous fantasy of the poet and the
artist: a woman who loved him, a woman dressed in
mad clothes, set against strange effects of the light
and a singular play of colours, an extraordinary
woman painted by Rembrandt, his god. A shamelessly ostentatious woman whose eyes glowed with
that indefinable expression, that almost melancholy
fervour, of Van Ryn's masterpiece, the woman in the
square room at the Louvre. He desired her like that,
with skin the colour of amber, and even a spot of
rouge on her cheeks and of ash-blue under her eyes;
and he wanted her with a subtle and knowing mind,
demanding that she be extravagant and disturbing at
the right moment, but prudent and devoted the rest
of the time. This impossible dream, this taste for
the unrealisable, this greedy desire for feminine dis-
cretion and spontaneity regulated by the clock, tormented him. Marthe had seemed to him, with her
wild mane of hair, her dancing eyes and hungry lips,
to fulfil the ideal he had pursued in vain. He had
admired her on the stage, by turns provocative and

naïve, and he counted as much on the actress as the mistress to play the part he had assigned to her in their liaison.

He was thinking about all this. Then he suddenly remembered that the armchair wasn't where he should be, and he went into the bedroom.

Marthe fell asleep in a state of astonishment. She who had been a compliant slave to everyone, had never seen a man like him before; his amazing fervour, his lively youthfulness, his words of enthusiasm, his mad lyricism and his unbridled respect, all captivated her. She told herself that those in love were probably like this and she was grateful that in bed he did not remind her of her previous experiences. She who had guided so many travellers to Cythera, at so much per visit, forgot to make comparisons. Léo was truly her first lover.

At dawn the next morning, the young man looked at her and had a moment of doubt: she was still asleep, mouth open, legs bent, bare breasts, and everything on show. He asked himself if he shouldn't send her packing like the rest of them. But when he withdrew his hand, which had slipped under Marthe's head, she opened her eyes and smiled so sweetly that he kissed her and asked if she had slept well. Her only reply was to enfold him in her arms and kiss him on the lips, lapping his mouth like a cat. He lost his head.

He decided that she was worthy of all his affection and all his devotion, but what disconcerted him a little was the way she got up in the morning. She dressed like all whores, sitting on the edge of the bed, pulling on her long mauve stockings, buttoning her boots with a hairpin, drawing her chemise down over her legs and, finding herself next to the wash-stand, she did as they all did: drew back the curtain of the casement window and looked down into the courtyard. What woman had not made that same expression? What woman had not asked the same stupid question: 'Have you got any soap? Look, some face powder! Oh, what a lovely smell! It's *maréchale* hair-powder isn't it?'

He reproached himself for having believed she was different from the others, and yet, when she sealed up again in her dress all the treasures she had drawn out the night before, he felt something like regret. It pained him that she was going: he pressed her to stay for lunch. She was expecting her laundress, she had to get back home early. This reply exasperated him. Every woman who wants to get away is always expecting her laundress, he knew that only too well! She relented, however, and while she took off her hat and undid her wrap, the poet shouted down to the concierge in the courtyard.

Romel – that was his name – raised his head and solemnly barked out: 'I'm just coming.' He came up an hour later.

'See if you can find me a couple of steaks,' Léo said to him, 'a pie, some cheese, a cake and two bottles of Moulin-à-vent.'

'Right-oh.' And leaning over with a confidential air, Romel whispered into Léo's ear: 'Tell you what, I've just bought a stunning Louis XVI mirror, I could let you have it cheap.'

As unlikely as it might seem, Romel, concierge and cobbler by trade, had painted seascapes in his youth. If you believed him, he had 'a gift for it'. Now, he hawked around piles of junk, attempting to sell them to his tenants, above all in the morning when he knew they weren't alone. He could weigh up the charm and delicacy of their night-time companion by the tone of their refusal – because they all turned him down without exception. This particular morning, Léo said 'No' gently. He immediately concluded that the woman Léo had brought home would be a regular visitor and would ask him for the key to the premises, and he made a note to himself to bow very low when she left.

While Romel went on his way to the wineshop on the corner to order their lunch, Léo lit a big vinewood fire, and whenever Marthe, who was sitting on the fireside stool, raised her head a little, he planted long lingering kisses on her neck, lips and eyelids, which closed and trembled under the hot breath of his mouth. He was thinking of the exploits of Hercules the killer of monsters, the son of Jupiter and Alcmena, when Romel came back, followed by a boy who carried the food and drink wrapped in a cloth. He laid the table and left. Léo and Marthe sat opposite each other; she ate heartily, while he, not moving, listened to the gentle rhythm of her jaws; water whistled in the kettle, she poured it onto the coffee; then they sat closer together and in between the susurration of their kisses, the water sputtered as it dripped through the filter. On the floor below, a pianist was knocking out a tune from *Faust*. From

outside, the voice of a beggar-woman, alternating
with the tinkling of the piano, rose up in the wintry
silence, extolling the glory of love and the unforgettable victories of 'Cupid's arrow'. They were numb
from the heat of the fire; neither of them could
summon the energy to open the window and throw
the woman a *sou*. They started to doze off listening
to this monotonous song; but then she got up,
stretched herself, kissed him and, after arranging
to meet him that same evening at the theatre, she
hurried off.

He felt lonely as soon as she had gone through the
door; his rooms seemed bleak and cold. He put on his
hat and coat and went out. He needed to kill some
time. He renewed his pursuit of a publisher who
owed him some money: he couldn't extract a single
sou from him. Then he wandered along the boulevard
and went into a café; three o'clock was striking on a
round wall clock perched above a shelf of bottles. He
assigned himself the task of sitting there on the
banquette for an hour. He read and re-read all the
papers, yawned, lit a cigar, remarked that the people
around him were engaging in idiotic conversations;
that two pot-bellied individuals, one of whom had a
harelip and the other a squint, were laughing like
drains as they played billiards; he looked at the clock
again, called to the waiter, who came over too
quickly for his liking, and then he left, reproaching
himself for not having waited another five minutes
more until the clock struck four.

He sauntered along, looked at the shopfronts,
threaded his way down an alley, smiled at a little girl

skipping with a rope, strode along at double speed as far as the Bastille, ignored the little sprite cutting a caper on top of his column, retraced his steps, and went into another café, ordered an appetizer, re-read the newspapers which he knew by heart and then left again. At the top of the Rue Vivienne, he was glad to meet a friend he usually avoided; he offered him an absinthe, but as soon the hands pointed to six o'clock, he hurriedly left him.

The moment was approaching when he would see Marthe again. He dined badly, feeling neither hungry nor thirsty; he ran all the way to the Rue de Fleurus and made his way to the green-room where all the actors were gathered.

It was the first night. Ginginet was more bad tempered and grumpier than usual this evening. His pins were killing him, he said, tapping his legs. What's more, he was fuming with resentment, he had lost three games of bezique and the fourth wasn't looking too good either because his opponent, Bourdeau, had just declared 250 and as he also had the two aces of trumps in his hand all hopes his adversary had of revenge were shattered at a stroke.

Ginginet muttered, his nose in his cards. 'Forty for the knaves,' he shouted furiously as he threw down four Jacks on the table; he got up for a moment to look through a peephole in the curtain at the audience they had that evening.

He came back exasperated.

'All porters and lamplighters,' he announced, 'with a few dandies and tarts in silk into the bargain. There's only one well-groomed thoroughbred in the whole house, and he's pockmarked, a right attic-load of freckles! Ah, I tell you it makes me sick playing to a bunch of faces like that. By the way, suppose we count aces and tens?'

'I'm only in for 20,' sighed Bourdeau.

'And I'm in for 500,' grumbled Ginginet, 'I'm cooked! Hey, tell me Marthe my little gigolette, what's become of that pen-pusher who took a fancy to you? Do you still love him, you little minx? Oh, come on, don't pull a face like that, you know I'm only joking. Look, how about having a cup of coffee and a glass of the ol' cough medicine with us, how's that sound?'

'On stage! On stage!' yelled the stage-manager.

'Go to the devil!' barked Ginginet angrily.

But as the curtain was going up, the old actor had to conceal his bad temper and make his entrance.

Léo, who had just arrived, kissed Marthe and hid behind one of the flats.

The play fell flat. Apple-cores flew, owl-like tu-whit-tu-whoos drowned out the noise from the orchestra pit made by two sad old baldies who were scraping the bellies of their cellos. Marthe and Léo took flight. It was every man for himself. The curtain fell. No one was left on stage apart from Ginginet and the two authors of the play, who looked at each other, crushed.

The actor consoled them with a few wise words.

'Young men,' he said, 'the profession of dramatic author may not provide you with bread, but at least it'll grant you plenty of apples. This lot will serve to make a nice apple turnover. As for my opinion on your work, here it is: those who hooted the play were right, those who bombarded me with missiles were dunces. And now, sound the trumpets, I'm off!'

CHAPTER V

Marthe got into the habit of spending every night at Léo's. She even ended up bringing half her wardrobe, not wanting to get up so early whenever it was raining in order to go home and change her clothes.

For a whole month, they imagined they were in love, then, one fine day, a double catastrophe crashed down on them. The theatre went bankrupt, and the newspaper Léo wrote for suspended his pay.

The poet lost a hundred francs worth of copy in this débâcle, and Marthe found herself out on the street, homeless.

She wept, said that she didn't want to be a burden to him, that she would look for another job, that, in any case, Ginginet was her friend and whatever theatre took him on would surely engage her with him.

Léo, who detested the actor and felt a mad urge to slap him when he was too familiar with Marthe or bullied her with his working-class civilities, told her flatly that he would never agree to her seeing Ginginet again.

'What's to be done then?' she sighed.

He shrugged that he didn't know. Deep down, though, both of them had the same thought and each was waiting for the other to propose it before accepting it at once.

He couldn't afford the expense of two rents. It

was necessary to find a means to pay only one. Their expenses would therefore by reduced by half. They could economise on restaurant bills and the cleaning woman: Marthe would take care of the cooking, keep the apartment clean, and wash and mend Léo's laundry; if need be, she could sew her own dresses and make her own hats. Léo ended up convincing himself that the two of them could live together more cheaply than when he was alone.

Once this plan had been decided, the poet couldn't rest until it was put into execution. He urged her to pack her bags, he borrowed money to pay off her bill at the hotel where she was living, he nailed things up and nailed things down, he rearranged everything completely at his flat so that she could install all her things. Their first evening together was beyond compare: Marthe re-established order in the house, cleaned out the drawers, put all the linen that needed to be repaired on one side, dusted the books and pictures, and when he returned for dinner, he found a good fire, a lamp that wasn't smoking as it usually was, and, in his armchair, turned with its feet to the fire and back to the table, a pleasantly dishevelled woman waiting for him.

'How well I'll be able to work,' he said to himself, 'now I'm so comfortable at home!'

Meanwhile, his money galloped away from him as if given free rein. Every day there was a new expense: wineglasses, a decanter, a few plates; he began to get alarmed, but he consoled himself by repeating that a job worth two-hundred francs a month was being held for him at a new magazine; the thing was to be patient; in a few months his situation would be better.

The paper died before it was born, poverty came and, along with it, the terrible disillusionment of cohabitation.

In the early days, each tried to be congenial; it was a case of who could anticipate the desires of the other and accede to them most unselfishly. It is common knowledge that the first argument breeds those that follow, but poverty is a sobering thing and, thanks to it, the wine of love was quickly soured. Léo started to see things more clearly. Besides, he was harrassed by a thousand of those little trifles that wear one down over time. Why was she so obstinate in not wanting to leave his armchair in front of his desk? Why this mania for reading his books and dog-earing the pages? And what's more, why this stubborn determination to hang up her dressing-gowns and petticoats on top of his overcoat and trousers, especially when she could have hung them on another hook and not forced him to lift off a whole cart-load of linen in order to get to his jacket? He also had to put up with the smell of her cooking, the heavy odour of wine in the sauces, the sickening stench of onions fried in a pan, and look at bread-crumbs all over the rugs and bits of cotton thread all over the furniture; the sitting room had been over-turned from top to bottom. On cleaning days it was even worse. The ironing-board had to be balanced across his desk and another table, and the washing had to be dried on a clothes-horse in the hall. The puddles of water on the parquet, the stale smell of lye, and the steaming laundry that left damp-stains on his brasswork and tarnished his mirrors, reduced him to despair.

These annoyances which were repeated every day, the absence of his friends which the presence of a woman kept away, the impossibility of working next to a mistress who, having nothing else to do, wanted to talk and tell you all the tittle-tattle of the building, the insolence of the concierge who having lost the job of cleaning the flat revenged himself by continual interference, the fact that Marthe sensed this hostility against her and insisted her man sort him out and make him stop, the resentful look on her face when he went out in the evening on business, or when, pressured by work, he read or took notes in bed, her complaints about the state of a dress that was past mending, that sigh which said all too clearly, at the sight of a threadbare shirt, that he must get some new ones in the next few days, and finally her determination to complain when there was no money and to give him a bad dinner whenever she'd bought herself some new gloves – all this exasperated him.

And besides, what advantages had he gained since he had lost his liberty? What had become of her long dresses, her flouncy petticoats, her black silk corsets, all the feminine artifice he adored? The actress and the mistress had disappeared, only the maid-of-all-work remained. He no longer even had that pleasure of the early days of their liasion, when he could think to himself on the way home: 'This evening, she's coming!' The hurried footsteps in order to

70

arrive home early, the anguish that oppresses you
when the hour of the rendezvous has passed and you
still can't hear her coming up the stairs and stopping
in front of your door. Ah, all that seemed so long ago.
No more good conversations by the fire with his
friends, no more intelligent discussions about this or
that book, this or that painting. Try and talk about
literature and the fine arts in front of a woman who
yawns into her hand, who furtively looks at the
clock, who seems to say to you, 'Can't you hurry up,
so we can go to bed!' That suicide of the intellect
that is called 'living together' started to weigh heavily on him.

She, for her part, was not much happier. She found
him cold, more occupied with his art than with her;
she rebelled against his sulks and his silences. They
each accused the other of ingratitude. Léo imagined
that he had made a great sacrifice in sharing his life
with Marthe, while she was convinced that she
had martyred herself for him. She did everything,
scoured the furniture, washed the floors and dishes,
laundered his linen; she saw none of her old friends,
whom he had politely turned away and, in exchange
for all that, she had no money! She couldn't even buy
a dress!

Moreover, she quickly grew tired of everyday
work, the housework was swept to the devil, the
meals prepared at random; she'd have a bit of rabbit
or some slices of roast lamb sent up from the nearest
chophouse. Léo complained.

'And where's the money?' she would say.

And when he retorted that it was cheaper to cook

at home than to go searching for meals, ready cooked, outside, she would moan, say she was worn out and wanted only to be allowed to sleep. She didn't even clear away the table, but undressed with an exhausted air and lay stretched out on the bed, every quarter of an hour asking her lover, who was still working: 'Aren't you coming to bed yet?'

He would respond by groaning; and then, tired of this battle, he would leave his work and go and lie down. But then she wouldn't budge, would pretend to be asleep, barely making room for him at the edge of the bed, forcing him to make his place between bed and wall; she would obstinately turn her back on him, drawing her legs away if he moved his closer to warm them up. Losing his patience, he would extinguish the lamp and try to sleep.

These childish tricks, these feminine sulks irritated him, and as they were repeated every time she went to bed alone, he ended up giving in to her and, in order to have a more companionable mistress, he had to sleep at ridiculous times. Even so, Marthe wasn't grateful; finding that he lacked will-power, she vowed to turn his weakness to her own advantage on the first occasion that arose.

On top of all this he was jealous, and following an argument caused by mud stains on her dress, which quite clearly betrayed the fact that in spite of her denials to him she wasn't staying at home all day, their life together became unbearable.

She would go out while he was correcting proofs in some newspaper office or foraging through old books in the library, and then deny having put a foot outdoors; he obviously couldn't tie himself down watching her all the time, but sometimes he checked the housekeeping book, looking to see if the velvet ribbon or the hat she had bought were written down. He added up the receipts over and over again, fearing that these purchases had not been included, asking himself if the allowance he gave her had been completely spent on household necessities and, if so, what money she could have used to make these new acquisitions.

Then without warning her absences ceased; she refused, with a tenacity he could not overcome, to go out with him in the street. He attributed this sudden change of mind to one of those caprices that women are prone to and which it would have been mad to oppose. For him to have understood the girl's obstinacy, he would have had to have known about her past and he knew only the scraps she had dished up in moments of considered reflection. The truth was that Marthe had seen some of her old friends again, and that, one day when she was particularly hard-up, she had posed to herself the daisy-petal question 'Do I love him a little, a lot, or madly?' and had replied: 'A lot.' But when it comes down to it, a woman can feel affection for a man and yet not be faithful to him – you see it happen every day. So she had been tempted to flirt with the czars of the local corn-market, rich men if ever there were any. She had almost pencilled in a rendezvous with one of them when she ran into a policeman who stared at her inquisitively.

Her status wasn't exactly clear. At any given

moment the police could get their hands on her; she had belonged to a brothel, she was an escapee; the detectives of the vice squad could take her back again.

She reached the point where she would start to tremble whenever the wind rattled the door or the water-carrier came plodding slowly up the stairs. She only went out now to get food – and then hurried back as quickly as possible. This life of fear and anguish didn't give her a moment's respite. She drank in order to forget her fears; she would drink rum by the glassful, squatting on an animal-skin rug in front of a blazing fire, and she would smile at the flames in a mute daze, shivering and running her hand over her forehead in a gesture of exhaustion; the terrible heat of the coals numbed her, her head spun, her will-power sagged along with her body, it was if she had been bound up and couldn't move her arms or legs, she would doze and swoon drunkenly in front of a roaring coal fire that scorched her face. Sometimes, instead of the torpor she yearned for, a fever gripped her, and with it came hallucinations and long periods of prostration from which she would wake, shattered and feeling like death. As a result of this carry-on, her reason would wander, and her head, after nodding grotesquely on her chest, would fall heavily onto her raised knees and she would remain in this position, inert, stupefied, until Léo arrived and, opening all the windows, angrily drag her over to get some air.

His patience was wearing thin. After a day which she spent stumbling against the furniture, battered

and almost blinded by an atrocious neuralgia, he
threw every bottle he could find out the window. She
stared at him with the resigned look of a whipped
dog, then she got up and, bursting into tears, held
him tightly, begging his forgiveness, promising not to
be ill again, and to make his life happy.

One evening he came home, picking up a letter
that the concierge, tired of waiting for him, had slid
under his door. He went over to the lamp, opened the
envelope, and turned dreadfully pale, two large tears
sprang to his eyes.

Marthe burst out sobbing. When she heard that
her lover's mother was seriously ill she had an attack
of nerves that left her prostrated, trembling and distracted on the bed. He was touched by this excess of
sensibility. It was, if the truth be told, more a trick
of her strained nerves than genuine emotion, and yet
at the word 'mother' she had felt something like a
blow to her breast. Her childhood, about which she
tried never to think, had suddenly come back to her,
her mother was no longer dead, she could see her
again leaning over her cradle, kissing her hands when
they came out from under the coverlet, smiling at her
with tears in her eyes when the room was cold. An old
refrain her mother had sung to her came back in
snatches; she tried to recall the rest but the strain of
remembering left her shattered, and she slept in a
deep sleep until the next morning.

When she awoke her lover was already up and
ready to leave. She kissed him effusively, promised to
write to him, wanted to accompany him as far as the
railway station, but he was already late. In the time

it would take her to get dressed, he would certainly miss his train. She had to give up her plan.

When Léo had gone, she hurriedly pulled on her skirt. She felt the need to walk, to get some fresh air; she considered her recent fear of the police crazy, and, going from one extreme to the other, she wanted to find herself in front of them, to snap her fingers at them, tell them to their faces, 'You're nothing but a lot of filthy narks,' but this state of over-excitement subsided as soon as she got outside.

She went to see one of her friends who worked as a waitress in one of the lowest dives in the Rue de Vaugirard. The saloon was almost empty when she went in and hadn't even been swept yet. The mirrors on the walls, smeared with pommade from the heads that continually leaned against them, were clear at the top and tarnished at the bottom; the floor, powdered with rouge, was starred with dried spit, phlegm, cigar butts and pipe dottle, the marble table-tops were ringed with tacky stains from dirty glasses, and, at the back of the room on a sofa, a living image of infamy, lay the landlady's father, whose job it was to work the beer pumps.

The room smelt of stale tobacco, an odour peculiar to bars. The old man snored as he dozed and Maria, Marthe's friend, sat on a banquette, her mouth hanging open vacantly. After they had kissed, Maria, dragging Marthe off into the kitchen, hurriedly said to her:

'Didn't you get my letter?'

'No.'

'But the police are on your tail, my dear. It was the

little redhead who told me; yesterday evening you were recognised by a police spy who had lost track of you, but who just happened to see you again.'

She stood there, stunned. Her worst fears had been realised. The doctors from the anti-venereal dispensary would ask her to explain why she had run away. They would go to Léo's apartment; the concierge would learn everything and when Léo returned he would tell him who she was, and what kind of life she had led. She resolved never to go back home.

'I'd willingly offer to hide you for a few days at my place,' said the girl, 'but I don't live alone and my old man wouldn't like it. You'd be better off going to Titine's.'

'Where does she live?'

'Ah, I don't exactly know; she lives, so they tell me, near Les Halles, but I don't know the name or the number of the street. But stay here until night-fall, and we'll see later on. Between now and then you'll have time to think it over and come to a decision.'

The evening came and Marthe still couldn't decide what to do. Fearing the vice squad detectives, who rounded-up all the women they found in the dives of the *quartier*, she fled the bar and, not knowing where to hide herself, made her way along the quays as far as the Pont Neuf, repeating to herself, without actually believing it, that fate would be kind to her and that she would meet her friend on the way.

Having arrived at the bridge she felt so tired, so desolate, that she knelt on a bench in one of those semi-circles at the top of each pier. She stared, with tears in her eyes, at the eddies of water that lapped and swirled around the arches.

The water of the Seine that evening was the colour of lead, streaked here and there with the reflected light of the street-lamps. To the right, in a coal barge moored to an iron ring as big as a hoop, the shadows of men and women moved indistinctly; on the left, rose the flat level of the bridge with its statue of the King. Below, planted next to a café, a tree cut its flimsy outline against the slate grey of the sky. Further away, the Pont des Arts faded into the mists with its crown of gas-lights, and the shadow of its pillars melting into the river in a long black stain. A boat passed through the arch of the bridge, throwing up a puff of hot steam into Marthe's face, leaving behind it a long wake of white foam which died out little by little in the sooty waters. A fine rain began to fall.

Marthe was no longer thinking of anything.

She was staring into the Seine, without really seeing it. The rain fell heavier now in large drops that lashed her face. She awoke as if from a dream. The spectre of the police rose up before her, implacable; she leaned over the parapet, had, for a second, the idea of ending all her troubles, then she took fright and drew back terrified, wanting to run away, when an unspeakably drunk man grabbed her by the arms.

'Hey, Marthe! Now then! What are you doing looking at the Seine, with the rain pelting down and your coat all drenched?'

And Ginginet, noticing how pale she was, asked her if she was in a bad way.

She confessed to him that she had been that close to throwing herself in the river.

'What nonsense, girly,' the drunkard barked dramatically. 'Are you dying of hunger? Have you killed someone? Have you had a bust-up with a friend? Have you been picked-up in the gutter for insulting the armed forces? What have you done that you should be homeless and wanting to kill yourself? Come, none of that, Lisette,' the merciless joker continued, holding his cane like a rifle; 'even if you were Boney himself, I'd not let you pass!'

She didn't say a word.

'But my little goose,' the actor continued, 'what good would it do you to drown yourself? It'd be stupid, like every death, even those in the fifth act of a tragedy; now let's see, think about it a bit . . . can you see yourself on a slab in the morgue with your red hair and a green belly? Look, don't make me play the role of guardian angel in weather like this. I haven't studied the part yet. Come on, you'd be better off having a drop of the hard stuff with me, even though you're a lady who keeps the company of poets, come and down a glass of brandy. That's settled, isn't it? No? It's like talking to a block of wood; aren't you going to answer me? I bet it's the fault of that scoundrel you took as your lover. Has Monsieur Léo made you miserable? Well then, leave him!'

At the sound of her lover's name, Marthe started to sob.

'Oh great,' groaned the drunkard, 'here's even more water now! Cover your glasses everyone!'

79

'Look!' she shouted, getting more worked up the more she cried, 'you'd have done better to let me die. Believe me, I've thought about it enough! You know how it is, you lose your head for a moment, you think it's all very simple to climb up on to a parapet and jump. That doesn't last long, let me tell you. You get a right fright, up there. It churns your stomach, that boiling water under the bridge; it's as if you're being gripped by the throat, being strangled. And that's stupid as well, because it would be better to finish it all quickly than to continue to live like I'm doing! Don't you see, Ginginet, you can say what you want, but Léo is a good boy all the same. I've behaved like the worst of women with him. I'd get sloshed you know, and he'd put me to bed, and he looked after me when I was ill. Would you have done that? You? you'd try to get pissed on what was left in the bottle. As for what you think of me, I don't give a damn. Between people like us there's no such thing as love. We meet someone and sleep with them, just like we eat when we're hungry. Oh, I've had enough of this life of continual fear, I've had enough of being hunted like an animal. I'll give myself up. And what if I do? When you first looked at me with your startled eyes the day you accosted me in that bar, didn't you think you'd found a virtuous one? You picked up a filthy tart, my dear. And you know, it's no good trying to clean it off, it sticks with you forever, comes back like an oil stain on a dress. And anyway, when all's said and done what's that to me? Neither father nor mother nor good health, that's called good luck when you do what I do.'

'Look,' she continued, poking her boot into some horse-shit, 'there's some dirt for you! Well, that's nothing. I'm in it up to my neck, and I swear to you I'm not going to lift my head up again, my friend, I'm going to sink in it until, mouth open wide, I choke on it and die!'

'Oh, but she's delirious,' Ginginet said to himself, startled to see her hurrying away towards Les Halles. 'Damn it, no more jokes, I'd better go after her!'

He almost caught up with her at the street corner; unfortunately his legs seemed formidably heavy, the noble vine had played havoc with his muscles; he had to stop and breathe, tuck in his shirt which was escaping from his trousers and waistcoat, and then run again the whole length of the street, one moment losing sight of her amid a mass of cabs, the next seeing her in the distance; he shouted after her, at the risk of getting himself arrested by the police.

Then he realised he was running along almost barefoot; his boots had given up the ghost in the course of this dizzying pursuit. Flaking off like pastry, flapping like a bellows, they got bogged down in a pile of manure, lost their grip, and their owner fell flat on his face.

He got to his feet, stunned by the blow and, with a doggedness that owed more to the tenacity peculiar to the drunkard than to the affection he felt for Marthe, he started off again in pursuit. In the distance, he saw her pull open a door and disappear. Bruised, bedraggled, puffing, and dripping with sweat, he arrived in front of this door, raised his head and looked up at the house; he stood there with

81

mouth open, lifted his arms to the heavens, let go of his cane and, stifled by drunkenness, suffocated by the stupor he felt, he stuttered:

'Oh, Lord Jesus! Well, here's a fine mess!'

And he fell headlong on to a heap of green cabbage stumps and endive leaves that studded the pavement of the street.

CHAPTER VI

He was surprised to wake up the next morning in a cell. He tried to recall what crimes he could have committed. Not coming across any, he concluded judiciously that he must have been sozzled; suddenly, he remembered having met Marthe, having followed her as far as a little side-street, the name of which escaped him. 'I must have imagined it,' he said to himself, 'it's impossible.' However, as he knew Léo's address, he resolved to go to his house as soon as he was released.

Indeed, he was bailed out that same day by one of his friends and he ran off as quick as he could in search of Marthe. The concierge informed him of her disappearance and the visit by the police. While they were talking, Léo appeared, getting out of a cab and holding a suitcase in his hand.

He barely acknowledged Ginginet, who said to him with an air of dignity:

'Monsieur, if you wish to have news of Marthe, you would do well to address yourself to the Prefecture of Police – second bureau, first division, Department of Public Morals – and they will give it to you. As for myself, if I mourn the loss of the actress, my former pupil, I'm full of admiration for the woman, my former mistress. She has at least one advantage over the others, she's given up deceiving men. Marthe will lie no more, now that she no longer has to simulate the moans and groans of true love.

What the bourgeois would call wallowing in the mire, or descending the ladder of depravity to the lowest rung, I myself call an expiation, a return to honesty!'

And so saying, more dignified than ever, the old ham raised his felt hat, which after the shocks and bumps of the night before was pitifully crumpled and resembled an accordion about to play a funeral march, and his droll and dilapidated silhouette hastily disappeared round the corner of the passage.

CHAPTER VII

After he'd left to see his dying mother, Léo had given little thought to Marthe. He adored his mother and the imminent danger she seemed to be in, which he feared he could not ward off, absorbed him completely during the train journey.

He stayed by her side for several days; the danger evaporated, his anxieties ceased, and then thoughts of Martha began to obsess him relentlessly. Did he really love her? He didn't even know himself. This girl had certainly captivated him more than any other. Before they had actually lived together, before they had come to know the drawbacks of communal life, he had felt violently enamoured of her. But after a week of intimacy, all that sense of freshness that a woman brings, which is admittedly very enchanting but which is the result of nothing more than cleverly arranged absences, all that was over, and all those hideous natural failings which everyone tries to ignore and overlook as far as the other is concerned, all were now exposed to view and she no longer presented that sense of mystery without which every passion tires. Those lustful instincts that are seasoned by feminine artifice were exhausted; after having tasted the exotic dishes of the high table, he'd been initiated into the mysteries of the kitchen and his appetite had disappeared at the same time as his desire to touch those subtle and invigoratingly spiced foods. He began to get bored of this monotonous duet played repeatedly, without hope of respite, in every domestic key. Besides, when he came to think about it, this girl had made his life unbearable with her mad desires and rages, her vicious drunkenness and her sickly despondencies, her sensual cravings that alternated with a barely concealed frigidity. If he had left Paris for any other reason except that which had called him away, he would have considered this escape as a schoolboy considers the holidays that have delivered him from the subjection of his masters.

The life of idleness he led at his mother's little house drove his thoughts back to Paris. He remembered the happy dinners, the childishness of those early days, the treachery of those struggles fought with kisses. From a distance, all his idol's faults faded away; he saw her, so to speak, idealised and more beautiful than she had ever seemed; the poet was reborn in the lover, he restored to a goddess' pedestal the doll under whose rosy-pink skin he had once glimpsed the stuffing; in short, he was dying of longing to worship her again.

Added to which he was riddled with anxiety. All his letters to her had remained unanswered and he was afraid something was wrong. He couldn't concentrate, he felt bored everywhere. Now that his mother was cured, there was nothing holding him any longer in the country. So he left.

The train journey, so tiring when it takes a whole day, increased his desire to see Marthe again still more. Vainly, he tried to kill time on that interminable day, forcing himself to take an interest in the movements of trains, in the machines that went by in a red mist of steam, in the reflections of sun on copper, in the rails that gleamed like thin streams of water, but he thought only of Marthe; he stared at the people squeezed into the compartment and amused himself for a few seconds looking at their faces and their ragged clothes. They were, for the most part, peasant men and women; an artist would have had a field day with this collection of noses: bulbous noses, retroussé noses, crooked noses, broken and flattened conks; there was a whole exhibition of teeth of every kind, white, yellow, blue, black, stumps of all shapes, some sticking out over lips, others beating a retreat into the gums. He even took out his notebook and tried to sketch the necks of peasant women who had their backs turned to him, fleshy necks covered with knobbly bumps like a chicken's or the skin of a Caribbean native, but he was soon bored, put his pencil back in his pocket and, sticking his head out of the window, stared at a long string of houses and trees which seemed to be joining hands and dancing a gigantic farandole in front of his eyes.

Then he fell back into his gloomy thoughts. The Gare du Nord finally loomed up out of the steam, he disembarked, jumped into a cab, and pulled up in the courtyard, heart beating, but after he had seen the odious Ginginet, he collapsed into an armchair overwhelmed by all he had just come to learn.

He looked around his room, which was just as it was the day he had left. Ankle-boots, their points in the air, heels on the ground, were stranded amid the flowers of the carpet; the bed was unmade, the jumbled sheets a mass of creases, the quilt stuffed and squeezed into the space between bed and wall, pillows flattened, corners sticking up. Everything spoke of a hurried exit, the hair-pins in a cup, slippers buried in every corner, a camisole hanging over the back of the armchair, a bowl full of soapy water, the musty smell, the scent of *Eau de Botot* mouthwash with which she'd cleaned her teeth, the subtle odour of *Chypre* perfume escaping from a badly stoppered bottle. All this chaos of objects, this assortment of smells, brought her unforeseen flight sharply to mind. He stood up as if worked by a spring and, at the sight of that bed in which all Marthe's tenderness and all her wicked charms had been encamped, he choked, standing motionless, his eyes staring stupidly at the tangle of sheets.

The days that followed were excruciating. He led the life of those who are stuck in Paris without family, without friends, and who, when it is time to eat in the evening put on their boots and go and search for fodder in some cheap eating house. Those rooms where groups of people in their Sunday-best come to eat insipid, pallid meat, the commotion of the waitresses in grey weaving between the marble tables, those miserable little carafes of wine, those cheap porcelain plates, the gluttony of idiots who spend two francs on food and eight francs on de luxe wines, the inexpressible sadness evoked by an old woman in black, alone, hidden in a corner and chewing a bit of boiled beef in slow mouthfuls, all those nauseating aromas, all those deafening shouts, all the elbowing of the crowds – for several months he experienced it all. He would leave the feeding trough disgusted and tired, not knowing what to do, irritated by the happiness of others, oppressed by a persistent boredom; then he noticed at the corner of some a street square, a figure, a dress which looked like Marthe's and it would be like a punch in the chest; he would return home and, shoulders hunched and legs crossed, try to write a few lines, then throw down his pen in anger, take up a book, look at his watch, waiting until ten o'clock chimed so that he could go to bed.

The days were hard enough to bear, but the nights . . . with the half-light of dusk and those red skies of autumn that are enough to drive anybody to melancholy, all his bitterness would revive and assail him more doggedly than ever. Whatever he wanted to do, he thought of Marthe; he saw her, sly and alluring, he recalled the rise and fall of her haunches on the sofa, she would smile at him, eyes aflame, open-mouthed, and he would get up, his senses stirred, grab his hat and rush out into the streets.

To all these sufferings were added those terrible trivialities of life that can break the proudest of men. It was these little things – the shirt in tatters one hadn't mended, the missing buttons, the frayed trouser-legs that gave you the air of a down-and-out – these foolish trifles that a woman magics away with a wave of her needle, that harassed him with a thousand pin-pricks and made him feel how totally abandoned he was by everyone. For the first time in his life he considered marriage, but as he had no job, he couldn't realistically think of such a prospect.

He reproached himself for not having kept track

of Ginginet, for not having asked him for Marthe's address; and he would search vainly for him in all the cafés he usually frequented. Then one evening as he was pounding the pavement, he was tapped on the shoulder by one of his friends, an intern at the Lariboisière Hospital. He told him about his misfortunes, asked him, on the off chance, if he knew where the old ham lived.

'But of course,' said the other, 'Ginginet's set himself up as a wineseller in the Rue de Lourcine, only ... only he's on the point of going bankrupt, so if you want to find him, you'll have to hurry up and go see him.'

Léo grabbed the young man's arm and dragged him off without further ado down the meandering backstreets of the Gobelins district.

CHAPTER VIII

Following the Boulevard de Port-Royal to the left of
the Observatoire, after a few minutes' walk they
arrived at some steps, which disappeared under a
bridge and gave onto one of the most hideous streets
in Paris, the Rue de Lourcine. On one side there was
a stretch of waste-ground littered with buckets full
of rainwater, blocks of stone propped one against the
other, and wooden poles linked by twine, on which
faded and blotchy camisoles, blue overalls, bottle-
green corduroy trousers and other tattered rags
fluttered like flags; on the other side, opposite this
building site of stones, a line of cracked and tumble-
down hovels stretched out like a string of onions,
their collapsing zinc roofs stoved-in like bishops'
mitres. Here, there were workshops belonging to little tradesmen, jewellers in down-at-heel shoes, gold-
smiths in leather who restored old clogs, patched-up
boots and retailed soles of cork and straw; there were
greengrocers where you could buy milk and lead sol-
diers; there were general stores in which, separated
by glass partitions, lay heaps of shrivelled apples
with wrinkled skins the colour of amadou fungus,
dunes of blanched almonds, piles of sugar-candy,
Guillout biscuits, rounds of Gruyère cheese, pots
of jam, pink and orange, clear and cloudy, litres
of red wine, and big wooden drums in which the
liquefying flesh of aniseed-flavoured Géromé cheese
decomposed; there were cheap eating-houses with

window displays in which shrivelled fish turned brown
and fell apart, and bloody rabbits were framed by
a wall of lacklustre dishes and salad-bowls that dis-
gorged prunes wallowing in a mire of their own
juices.

Léo and his friend tried to orient themselves.
Neither of them knew the actor's exact address.
Finally, not far from the Rue de Lyonnais, they
noticed a tobacconist's shop which proudly displayed
in its window, above tobacco-pouches made from
coarse leather and pig's bladders, a cluster of white
clay pipes with bowls molded into the heads of
young girls and goats, of Turks and Zouaves, of
Greek gods and patriarchs. A chubby-faced young
girl who was weighing out plugs of tobacco pointed
out the house they were looking for, a house recently
daubed a lumpy pinkish colour, a bit like straw-
berries crushed in *fromage frais* or the dregs of wine
in plaster. And indeed it was there, behind a zinc
counter bored with tiny holes to drain off the wine,
that the singer gesticulated and warbled. Belly
wrapped in a black apron, arms bare, mouth crenel-
lated with stumps of teeth, snout as red as a kidney
potato, Ginginet, old ham and drunkard by taste,
publican and pimp by necessity, drank from four in
the morning till midnight with his customers, who
for the most part worked as rag-pickers or as tanners
preparing animal hides.

But these workers only came either in the morning
at the break of day, or in the evening at nightfall. So
the inn was nearly always empty between nine
o'clock in the morning and eight o'clock at night,

and apart from a gang of boozers who would come to feed on badly-prepared *andouillettes* and *tripes à la mode de Caen*, the big salon was deserted. By contrast, in the evening it was so full you couldn't move, but then the actor would slip away, leaving the bar in charge of a big lanky chap in a velvet skull-cap, a one-time usher who did the books and served the clients when necessary, and he'd rejoin his friends and cronies, a collection of singers and newspaper hacks in the other saloon, separated from the larger one by the kitchen. These associates had bottomless stomachs and yet would drink without a *sou* in their pockets; but you don't spend years declaiming on the boards, mouth like a chicken's arse and eyes bulging like billiard balls, without being affected by it, and when Ginginet found himself with them, he willingly gave them credit, as if nostalgic for his own former poverty, and even, when he had taken a drop too much, deploring the death of the uncle who had bequeathed him this bar.

His cronies didn't regret the change in his fortunes quite so much as he did; they helped him to drink his way through his fortune and he himself let them do it with a magnificent disinterestedness which doubtless came from his habit of drinking from dawn to dusk, and from dusk to dawn. It was with some difficulty, that evening, that he recognised Léo; he had knocked back so many in the kitchen, had drowned his spirits in such a huge lake of cheap wine that he was lurching like a ship in distress, taking in not water but wine on all sides; he tottered from the bar to the back room, and there, patting his paunch in a

93

deep stupor, he recited a string of sonorous words the meaning of which he did not understand, arguing for the thousandth time, repeating his drunken actor's theories till he was hoarse in the throat, addressing himself particularly to an unfortunate journalist, whose nose was almost touching the table and who cried in a doleful voice: 'Ginginet, you're as eloquent as the late Cicero himself, but you're boring me stiff!'

Léo managed to bundle the old drunkard into a corner and asked him if he had any news of Marthe. Ginginet sang at the top of his voice:

'She is my love, she is my life!'

Then, winking at the poet and slapping him on the thigh, he slurred: 'Well, my boy, that slapper's got you by the innards, eh? She has a bit of fun, that's clear, but you must admit she's got a face like a hairdresser's dummy, "Mam'selle Sidonie", with her black peepers and sun-bleached hair!'

'Hey, dickhead,' someone hooted, 'you can gabble away later. Serve us some drinks first!'

It was impossible for Léo to take up the conversation again where they'd left off. He got ready to leave, promising to return the next day, but all the exits were blocked by the sheer mass of bodies. A triumphant racket filled the saloon; a dozen or so individuals had rolled onto the floor, and were sleeping, knees in the air, while in all corners of the room drunken women, hair dishevelled, burned under ardent male glances and struggled in the arms of assailants trying to paw them. Léo and his friend had just reached the door when it burst open, hurling onto the parquet a fresh bunch of working girls out on a binge, shaking their petticoats, laughing stupid laughs, and shouting at the tops of their lungs:

'Can-can! Let's do the can-can!'

Léo thought he was going to faint. He had just recognised Marthe in this batallion of show-offs; she went terribly pale and waited for him. He stopped in front of her, his eyes blazing, his limbs trembling. He wanted to speak, but felt as if a hand was gripping his throat and, muttering, stuttering, mad with rage, he made that gesture of disgust with his arm that is peculiar to Parisians; then, pushed forward by his friend and deafened by the cries of the people he was jostling, he found himself out in the street without knowing how he got there.

After he had gone, Ginginet noticed that Marthe was wiping her eyes. He thought for a moment, then he called her over and took her up to her room, a miserable lath-and-plaster hovel, and crossing his arms he said to her:

'Well?'

As she did not reply, he started again, getting angrier as he spoke:

'Look, I've had it up to here with you! I dragged you out of the whore-house you were lying in, sprawled on your back, I got you struck off the books of the Prefecture of Police, I brought you back here, you stuff yourself, you drink, you smoke, that's everything you could want in life, that is! You've had the best luck any woman could wish for, and in exchange for this paradise, in exchange for all these drinks, in exchange for all these blow-outs, you play me for a sucker, you fleece me whenever you please! Well, it's infuriating and I'm not going to put up with it! I'm not getting my money's worth, I'm being short-changed, I ask for some meat and I get nothing but bones. No, it's really too much. You come, you go, you come back, you don't come back, I keep my mouth shut – I can't do anything else – you have other lovers, that's for sure, kids of twenty who keep telling you they love you and you believe them; you think you're eating turbot because it's written on the menu – as if they still served turbot! Idiot! It's flounder you're propping yourself up with, it's like all those things which should be truly worthwhile, they don't exist! It really is true that it's only faith that saves you . . . and stupidity. Oh, there's no point in glaring at me like that, you know, I see you clearly enough! I know you and your kind: you can have twenty-four lovers, one every hour, it's of no consequence to me – you're either on the game or not on the game, there's nothing more to say, it seems completely natural to me. But I don't want you as reserved with me as you are with the others. You understand me, don't you? And I don't want you to see your poet any more. If he were to get his claws on you again he'd not only have the woman, but the mistress. The woman, for a while maybe, but the mistress, never! Look, make up your mind, my girl, it's take it or leave it.'

'I'll leave it,' said Marthe.

'You'll leave it? Make yourself comfortable, then. Go back to him now, your down-and-out lover. No, listen . . . stay and think about it for a few minutes.

96

With him, it'll be unrelenting poverty; with me, your glass'll never be empty, a never-ending feast, stuffing yourself till your jaws ache.'

And as Marthe started to bundle up her clothes without even listening to him, Ginginet took her by the hands and continued:

'Look, perhaps I'm wrong after all, because when all's said and done it's not your fault he saw you this evening. Come on, trust me, let's not argue any more; besides, with all this talking, I feel like my gizzard's as dry as dust. I don't bear a grudge, and nor do you, isn't that so? What do you say, my dear, if we go and have a tot of *Bischof*? What do you think? I'll give Ernest a shout to bring us up a big bottle ... No? Aren't you thirsty? Oh, don't be scared, go on, it'll be a proper *Bischof* you'll be drinking, not one of the ones I serve downstairs; I'll make it with a bottle of Graves, that'll be nice, eh? Dear God, what do I have to do to make you smile? Let's see, put down your bundle, you don't need to carry it tonight. Besides, where would you go? Not to Léo's again ... Oh, damn and blast it, if you go there ...'

'Well, and what if I did? Oh yes, do you think I was listening to all that stuff you've been harping on about for the last half-hour? You got me out of my prison, that's true. And why? So as to plant me in a bar and warm up your drunken customers. I serve as the standard-bearer of your slop-house; I just act as a box of matches, but I don't have the right to burn in earnest. As for my down-and-out lover, as you call him, I *could* love him perhaps if he had a bit more fire in his belly, if he wasn't such a wimp, if he was a real

97

man. But, all the same, in spite of everything, I almost fell for him again this evening; he treated me with real contempt, and that stirred me. Ah! I can't hide it from you, I was on the point of going after him.'

'As if he'd have wanted anything to do with you!'

'Not wanted anything to do with me? Oh, but you're stupid aren't you? But then not all men pardon the women who make them suffer. If they did, there'd be no more unhappiness in the world and scarce any need for prisons and judges. As for you others, it's a good trick to keep you in the palm of our hands! Oh, it's very simple, that is.'

And almost touching him, she offered him her marvellous lips, as striking as poppies, burning against the white flame of her teeth.

Ginginet felt a stirring deep inside and he held out his arms.

'Take your paws me off, you old fool!' she said. 'I was play-acting, and it was you who taught me how. That's something never seen before, nor ever known: I got one over on you. You see, all things considered, your paunch offends me with its perpetual wobbling from side to side; and with your scrofulous cheeks and your bulbous nose, your face really doesn't do it for me anymore. Good night!'

'You know what, Marthe,' said Ginginet, going pale, 'I've got a raging desire to give you the slap you deserve.'

'What! You slap me? Don't come a step nearer or I swear I'll break this carafe over your head!

Ginginet did not wait for any more; he threw

himself on her, catching a corner of the carafe in mid-flight that dented his skull, but he grabbed the girl by the wrists and flung her roughly on to the floor.

She got up battered and bruised and looked at him more in surprise than in anger.

'You got what you deserved!' the actor said, 'now go to bed.'

And he left, double-locking the door behind him. He went downstairs, then slapped his forehead, came back up the stairs again, opened the door and said to Marthe: 'By the way, you know if you feel like going to find Léo again don't be embarrassed my dear!'

She didn't breath a word.

Ginginet muttered to himself: 'I've got her. Now that she's free to go and rejoin him, she won't move a muscle,' and stroking his nose he added sententiously: 'It's astonishing how stupid these poets are; they make up fancy phrases, they cry, they moan, they groan – as if that had any effect on women, they only love those who beat them! It's not cherry-brandy you should serve to whores, it's vinegar. Now, I've got a good week of loving to look forward to!'

CHAPTER IX

Ginginet was right. Marthe had reached a point where her senses could feel nothing but violent shocks. A fearful love, a love living only on brutality and abuse, a nervous system wound-up by excess and relaxing only under the weight of physical pain and the pleasures of degradation, the tender hatred one bears for the man who whips you, her angry revulsion against such bondage, and the exhilaration of striking her benefactor knowing she'd be crushed by him in return – all this rendered Marthe almost mad. She experienced moments of complete dejection and prostration, during which she received his blows without moving, until, screaming with pain she begged him not to kill her. There were also periods of reaction, days when, howling and rearing, she would launch herself on him, experiencing a bitter pleasure in grappling hand to hand, in rolling on the floor, in breaking everything that came within reach, and then, breathless, energy spent, lovesick and shy, she would wrap her bruised arms around the sinister joker, who would then go downstairs and knock back a drink, replying to the boozers who had been astounded by the outcry, 'Oh, that was nothing! I was just ironing my wife's chemise.'

One day he came down face covered in blood. Everyone in the room burst out laughing. Their jeers exasperated him; he went back up to her room and almost kicked Marthe senseless. They had to pull her out of his hands and throw her into a cab which dropped her off at the nearest hotel.

In a stroke she was cured of her love. When she awoke the next morning, battered, her face bruised by the blows, she wondered at herself for having put up with these shameful fights, and she felt a horrible disgust for the man who had beaten her like this. She still had a few *sous* in her pocket; she stayed in the hotel until the traces of these fisticuffs had disappeared, then she dressed in her best clothes and resolved to go and look for a place to hide with one of her friends, an ex-Bobino show-girl whose address she had found.

This woman had, since her thirty-fifth year, been kept by an old married man who consoled himself for the beauty of his wife in the debased charms of his mistress.

When Marthe arrived at her rooms, Titine, sprawled on a sofa, was having her palm read by her maid, who was explaining to her in her provincial Auvergne gabble the disasterous influence of the line of Saturn, and who was secretly surprised to find that a woman of so few morals didn't have more marks on her Mount of Venus. Marthe interrupted this seance of chiromancy and in a few words explained to her friend the favour she wanted of her.

'You fell in at the right time, my dear,' the tart said, 'there's a party here tonight. It'll be very amusing, you'll see. There'll be lots of rich young men and if you fancy I'll introduce you to one or other of them. You see, my child, it's no life for you to be going off with every Tom, Dick or Harry. It's really too much to have one man who keeps you and another who swindles you; you must make an end of it. Look at me, I'm very happy; for a lover I've a bit of an eyesore it's true, but he almost never spends the night – and that has to be taken into consideration. Do as I've done, bag yourself an old man who's already married, or a very young one who won't marry until after he's let himself be ruined; they're both equally worth getting. The main thing is not to take a lover who's past thirty. Neither love nor passion – men like that they're the death of women like us!'

The party that evening was delightful. The fat wholesaler arrived first, armed with a truffle paté and a basketful of wine. He was an amiable short-arse and a jovial host, this skirt-chasing merchant. Big-bellied and short of breath, he had bushy side-burns and his face offered that astonishing peculiar-ity, a nose the colour of aubergine, while the rest of his face seemed to be stained that striking red used by enamellists, Cassius purple. He paid slightly sug-gestive compliments to Marthe, explained to her that, two or three years ago, he had married a young girl, that they had been separated since he had met Titine – in bed if not in law – and he topped off his con-fidences with the admission that he adored youth and that his greatest happiness was to dine with happy-go-lucky boys and pretty girls.

The doorbell started to ring. Guests arrived in groups. Old men in formal attire, sporting lascivious smiles over their toothless lips, young men wearing wing collars, short jackets, baggy trousers and tas-selled boots, women of a certain age, rouge clashing

on talc, young girls with husky masculine voices and
flat, saggy chests, and some freshly-hatched schoolboys with centre partings and stripey socks – all
crushed into that tiny sitting-room. The uneasiness
of the first few moments quickly dissipated, the men
grew bolder, the fat businessman laughed his big
deep laugh. Titine assumed the supercilious air of a
society hostess, the maid was as familiar as a whore's
skivvy, the punch circulated and banal remarks
began to be exchanged. As yet, the women didn't
dare reveal themselves for what they were or give free
rein to their usual open-air-café boisterousness, the
older military-types were saving their energy for
feeding time, and the younger men were chatting
about last night's dance at Madame So-and-So's.
Then someone suggested they loosen their legs. The
quadrille started off fairly decently, but as the
couples warmed up and the fat man, incapable of
controlling himself, started to make salacious com-
ments, the dance rapidly degenerated. By supper-
time, the old men had unbuttoned their waistcoats
and were jigging up and down, their coat-tails in the
air and arms flailing, breathless, sweating, puffing,
beating their thighs, wobbling their stomachs.

The maid opened the door to the dining room.
Everyone rushed to the tables; they sat down pell-
mell, women on men's knees, and started picking at
the truffles and the *petits pois*. His paunch heaving,
his eyes roving, big daddy was exultant. He poured
glasses of champagne for the women, foaming pink
champagne, and he pressed his old satyr's lips to the
arms of the women sitting next to him. It was like a

signal. Couples drew closer together. Marthe was sitting next to a young man who was talking to her about horse-racing and about a bet he'd placed on Finette, 'a superb filly', as he put it.

When he had exhausted this subject of conversation, he muttered a few heavy-handed compliments to which she responded only with a smile, holding herself back in order to ask her friend who this dandy was.

'He's a first-class idiot,' Titine told her, 'stupid and rich; sharpen your toothy-pegs, my girl, and bite away. Be nice, but keep a tight rein on him – you have to with snotty-nosed brats his age!'

Then everyone got up from the table and went to drink coffee and liqueurs in the sitting-room. It was a proper stampede. Buried in their armchairs, the old men sat motionless: stuffed and drowsy, they digested their food. The young ones fluttered about and lit cigarettes; some, very pale, disappeared from view; others sat next to women and, showing off, began to tease them. Marthe became as cold as marble when her effete young man, emboldened by the free and easy behaviour of the other couples, tried to kiss her. He was a little bit surprised, but consoled himself, happy at having fished out of this filthy sink of iniquity a women who had a sense of decorum and wouldn't let herself get carried away on the first night.

'You're sleeping here tonight aren't you?' said Titine.

'But how can I?' Marthe replied, 'your lover's going to stay here tonight.'

'Him?' her friend said, pointing her finger at the old man who was lying unconscious on the sofa, redder and more bloated than ever, 'get away with you! He would really be too lucky if at his age and without danger to his health he could gorge himself on meat and wine like that and then spend the night with me afterwards!'

CHAPTER X

Less than a week had gone by before Marthe found herself in possession of a large apartment which she proceeded to furnish with appalling taste. To avenge herself for having had to eat with her fingers in the past, she wanted to have silver-plated cutlery, and among her other purchases she took care not to omit fake brass doorknobs, cheap rosewood furniture, mirrors with over-the-top gilt frames, and those ubiquitous wall-brackets with pink candles. Besides, her lover had no complaints; as long as his woman was eccentrically dressed and let herself be dragged off to fine parties and to the race-track, he was satisfied, added to which it delighted him to overhear kind-hearted people saying as they raised their eyes to the heavens: 'That little fool is on the road to ruining himself.'

The idea that he was capable of eating up his entire capital captivated him. Marthe was revolted by the ineptitude of the man. When he dragged along behind him a whole string of bearded wastrels, hair done-up like a tart's and steeped in opoponax, or when, sprawling in the sitting-room they jabbered on for hours, enthusing inanely over the glories of Tartine, who had beaten Jacinthe by a length, while Saxifrage and Mascara had been unseated at the starting post, she clenched her fists in anger.

She had, it's true, some distractions. The following Monday her lord and master brought home a couple of grave but considerably inebriated men who took her by the chin and said with an air of mystery:

'You know, don't you, that tomorrow the market will be very unsettled, wavering between the incentives offered by the government and a widespread distrust caused by the depreciation of foreign stocks?'

'Oh, I'm not so sure, what interests me more is to be assured that the Saragossa scheme is holding firm and that it'll yield excellent dividends.'

'Pah! Basically none of it's looking very bright; even if certain stocks are holding up well, it's a sad fact that the market is going down, because ultimately, except for our own bonds, on which there'll always be deals to do, the other shares have little to offer. I'm not speaking, of course, about railway shares, which look very promising.'

'Oh!' cried Marthe in disgust, 'I prefer the layabouts to this lot.'

Her lover thought her ill-bred, but he attributed this strange outburst to the two glasses of champagne she had drunk.

Marthe reproached herself for her rudeness and henceforth didn't say a word, bottling up her bitterness and her anger. Her lover had displeased her from the very first day; and she detested him from the very first night. He arrived home about two o'clock in the morning, a saucy gleam in his eye, his mouth stuffed with a fat cigar. He talked about the horse he was going to back in the next handicap, and, hitching up his trouser-legs with a fine semblance of absent-mindedness, he revealed to the woman he was keeping that he was wearing long pink tights. As she failed to go into ecstasies over this clownish elegance, he pulled a little at his leggings and, pouting his lips, said: 'Can you see how supple that silk is?'

She kept quiet, waiting for that commonplace courtesy, that ordinary civility which every man, however mean or stupid he is, displays – on the first night at least – to the woman he is supposed to be trying to conquer. She'd have had to wait for a long time. When he had finished his cigar and, with a stamp of his foot, ground the butt into the carpet, he murmured in a self-satisfied manner: 'I bet you can't guess what's in that bag? No? Ah, it's funny, women are never any good at guessing. Well, it's a nightshirt;' and with monstrous delight he showed off a belted nightshirt of Surah silk, trimmed with flaming red ribbons.

For the first time since she'd left him, Marthe thought of Léo. What a difference between the approaches of these two men. Where was the poet's ritualised sensuality, the restrained haste with which he undressed her? Léo would undo, one by one, her petticoats, then unlace her corset, the silk would rustle and flutter against her hips as he pulled on her nightdress, her unconstrained breasts swelling under the material, which shimmered from top to toe. Then he would pick her up and carry her to bed, stealing kisses as she swooned, her body supine in his arms. Doubtless the evening she had come home with him, those first few moments had been difficult, but once they they had taken each other in their arms, once they had warmed to the battle, what lively pleasures had they not tasted! The unforgettable memory of

nights from which she emerged with shoulders
covered in love bites and hair unkempt, the over-
whelming image of those times when his hands
wandered over her body, all those tender moments
together, all those breathless pleasures obsessed her
anew, and, angrily, she pushed her lover roughly into
the alcove and he bumped against the wall and
grumbled in his sleep: 'Oh, stop it, you know you're
really annoying me. Can't you keep still!'

He got into the habit of coming every day and
harassing her with his presence; she could have hap-
pily strangled him, this imbecile who looked at her
without moving a muscle when she was getting ready
for bed. She started to feel so pestered by this man
that she no longer even took pleasure in spending his
money; she stayed at home, lying in bed for days on
end, smoking cigarettes, drinking toddies, feeling
tired and weary. And this solitude she had created for
herself by foregoing visits to other women friends,
this drowsiness that never left her, was bound to end
up as it had before when she was living with the poet,
in appalling bouts of drunkenness. She downed huge
quantities of beer and spirits, but even as her mind
was clouding over with drink, she would see Léo's
room again: the lover she had tortured for the fun
of it was avenged by the persistent memory of his
kindness.

Marthe wallowed in wine in order to cheer herself
up and to banish forever her obsession with the poet,
but now her stomach rebelled and she had atrocious
burning pains in her belly. She was forced to stop
these binges and, one evening, exasperated at not

being able to sleep, convulsed by her sick nerves, she jumped out of bed, dressed, grabbed a cab and directed it to her former lover's house.

It was automatic, it was unconscious. The gusts of wind that came in through the windows of the cab brought her to herself. It was ten o'clock at night, she was on the point of stopping the cabman and getting out. She must be truly mad to go and see Léo like this. Did he still live at the same address, would he be at home, might she not find him with another woman? And then what kind of welcome would he give her? If she had returned to see him the day after their chance meeting at Ginginet's, no doubt he would have shouted at her, no doubt he would have humiliated her, but at the end of the day, wouldn't he have fallen into her arms? But by now, his anger would have passed, and with it the inevitable consequence: a tiredness of spirit, a weariness of heart; he would simply beg her to leave. Marthe was still hesitating when the cab stopped, then gambling everything in a single gesture she quickly rang the doorbell so as not to leave any time to retrace her steps, went up the stairs and, breathless, knocked on the door with her hand. The door opened and Léo looked at Marthe in astonishment and said:

'It's you!'

'Yes . . . well, I was just passing through the area, I came to see how you were . . . Is everything OK?'

'Yes, but . . .'

She put her fingers to his mouth and went on:

'Come on, don't say anything, don't let's talk about the past, what's done is done. Besides, I haven't climbed four flights of stairs to pick a quarrel with you. Look, let's talk about anything you like; are you working much; are you having fun, have you found a publisher?'

Léo looked at the door with an air of anxiety.

'Ah, you're expecting her,' she murmured, 'I should have guessed – I'm going now in any case – is she blonde or brunette?'

'Blonde and, what's more, decent.'

'Decent! So there are decent girls who come to a man's room at eleven o'clock at night! My God, she's just like the rest of us. More or less respectable when she walks, more or less enthusiastic when she strips off. And afterwards? Well, I want to see her, I'll rip off that sweet-little mask of hers I can tell you! You'll see if her decency doesn't just peel off. But I'm being stupid; it isn't any of my business whether she's decent or not.'

At that moment the doorbell rang. The young man made as if to answer it; Marthe felt that she would be lost if the door were opened and she stood in front of Léo and hung on his neck; he tried to disengage himself, but Marthe's eyes took fire, her lips burned him with their moist flames; panting and dishevelled, she dragged him over to the window. The doorbell rang more insistently.

'I love you,' she murmured, 'don't open the door; I'll fight her right now if she puts a foot inside here!'

He resigned himself, furious at having been tricked like this. The footsteps receded, the two lovers stared at each other without saying a word.

Marthe came and sat on his knees and kissed him;

111

he let her, but did not return her caresses; then, as if finally expressing an idea which had long been bothering her, she cried: 'Oh, men are all the same! Do you really think I love them, these men who are only interested in a woman for what they can get out of her. It's the done thing to carry one off and compromise yourself with her; that's all we're good for girls like us – to complain about living with such imbeciles, and to make them jeer because they hang around with tarts like us. And when they're tired of the way we look, it's 'Goodnight, and find someone else, my girl!' And they reproach us for going through their fortunes! But it's a war after all. You ravage and pillage. Look, you used to tell me about a woman – I can't remember her name, I'm not very educated for one thing – who was a statue. She came to life, you said, at the kiss of the man who made her; it's the opposite now: we become like marble when they kiss us. Ah! if you knew how tired I am of playing this charade. Look, it's not true that I came here by chance, I came here on purpose, I wanted to warm my feet against yours, and it may sound stupid to you, but there are days when it feels good not to have to spend the night with a rich man; and it's only natural after all to bite the hand that feeds you.'

He was no longer even listening to her; but she decided to conquer him again all the same; she grabbed his head between her hands and, covering it with kisses, she stormed him with a burst of rapid fire from her lips!

He slept badly, and when dawn broke he got up,

sat in an armchair and looked at the dozing girl, her hair pouring in a vermillion torrent over a ravine of white pillows. He had certainly had enough of her; she had revolted him ever since he'd found out how she made a living. Above all, he considered her contemptible, and yet how to avoid the snare of her eyes, how to escape the ambush of her mouth?

She turned over and, smiling, her head a little thrown back, her breasts heaving, her open nightdress revealing glimpses of white skin under a mist of Mechlin lace, she sighed softly. He looked at her, astonished at no longer feeling any desire for this woman he used to kiss; he now experienced nothing but shame, a kind of depression from having submitted to caresses she had no doubt lavished just as generously on all those she met on her rounds.

Certainly the woman he was seeing now was, as a mistress, inferior to Marthe. No mad bursts of energy, no turbulent carnal desires, but rather a profound tranquillity, an uninterrupted inertia. Léo had plucked her one evening just as she was about to wilt, and she had bloomed in his apartment with the indifference of a hardy perennial. She happened to be married and separated from a husband who had crushed her with blows of his fist, and yet whenever she thought about him her eyes filled with large tears and she wept over her fate, repeating that she would have loved to stay with him and have his children. The poet would have found her insufferable if she hadn't served as a kind of harbour, in which he could refloat his stranded ship. He had even ended up getting attached to the poor woman, who was so shy she never dared to raise her eyes and so uncoquettish that she wore a striped head-scarf in bed.

He regretted having opened the door to Marthe, and at that moment he was furious with her; he avoided looking at her now, but she opened her eyes and called him over to the bed. He was almost on the point of falling under her spell again, so fascinating was this tart with her bright eyes. But the daylight which filtered its gold-dust through the curtains showed him a face bruised by the depredations of the night, and a posture that revealed a whore who had been dragged through every gutter in the city. He didn't reply and whistled as he stared out of the window.

Marthe got up, dressed slowly and said to him: 'You were right after all: we're worn out, my dear. I thought we could rediscover our old happiness, but we haven't enough energy, either one of us, to bring it back to life; it would be better to end it and not see each other again. I'm going, and for good this time.'

She held out her hand; he couldn't stop himself from kissing her on the cheek, and then, more deeply moved than he wanted to appear, he let the door close behind her.

CHAPTER XI

Marthe returned to her flat, feeling faint and withdrawn. Her lover had waited for her all night and had prepared a series of reproaches for her return that were half-sentimental, half-mocking in tone. At the first words he uttered she looked him in the eye and said to him: 'Is the lease of this flat in my name?'

And when he replied 'Yes', she shouted: 'In that case, you'd better do me a favour and clear out now!'

He was astonished, stammered a few insults and then picked up his silk nightshirt and disappeared.

When he had left the room, she breathed a sigh of relief and, running to the cupboard, knocked back a big glass of kirsch in one gulp, then she angrily grabbed the neck of the bottle and drank straight from it.

This binge made her ill and more miserable than ever. A crowd of young men came to see her, offering to take their friend's place in her good graces; but she preferred to have them all rather than to endure one on his own, and so she resumed her old way of life, feeling no affection, no tenderness for all these men who queued up at her bedside, as if she had been burnt up by the fires of love. She even went so far as to take as lovers those vulgar men in baggy caps bearing at their temples that stigmata of infamy, the kiss-curl. But these latter disgusted her even more than the others and so she contrived to spend her nights alone.

So, behind her pale silk bed curtains, in an insomnia that she couldn't overcome, she dreamed of the past. She mourned for her little daughter who had died at birth, and almost came to love the young man who had cared for her during that horrible crisis; then as her pitiful life unfurled before her like the changing tableaux in a kaleidescope, she shuddered, measuring the depth of the mire into which she had sunk, and when she came to that period of her life when she had served in the regiment of love's mercenaries, then, in the silence of her bedroom, the spectre of the whore-house rose up in her mind's eye in all its gaudy finery and with its sinister cries of pleasure . . .

She'd gone in, confused, and the souls within, made charitable by drunkenness, said to her: 'Don't be afraid, you'll soon get used to it'; then they undressed her until the only thing she had on was a muslin slip, beneath which her body was an indistinct pink blur; they brought in glasses and she started to play cards for bumpers of foaming beer until the arrival of Monsieur Henri, the barber whose job it was to tart the girls up. When everyone had a mop of bouffanted hair on their heads and a mass of ribbons and flowers hanging over their foreheads, they drank absinthe, shuffled the cards again, and waited until it was time to set sail, whether for Lesbos or for Cythera. Finally, after dinner, everyone went down into the drawing-room where, standing in the doorway, Madame Jules kept a look-out.

Two, three, a score of people came in; they asked

for drinks, they went up to the first floor, then the bell would ring and all the girls would come tumbling downstairs, in a headlong rush, pushing, tickling and pinching each other, some making their theatrical tinsel swirl amid the red vapour of the gaslight, while others stood out, white and naked, against the imitation marble of the walls.

This went on until eleven o'clock, when the table was laid for supper and the whole squadron went back upstairs to stuff themselves with slices of saveloy, potted mince sandwiches and portions of rabbit stew, and then the bell would ring again. Everyone gulped down the morsel they had in their mouths, and, for the twentieth time, the girls would be engulfed in the tempestuous noise of the market-hall; then, except for one or two, they would go upstairs again only to return later, their stockings glinting with gold and silver coins.

But it was towards one o'clock in the morning when the frenzy reached its supreme intensity. Passers-by would crowd in; then the frolics and the capers, the stamping and shouting were incessant as the girls vied with one another in silliness and high spirits. Lips splashed with red lipstick, teeth scrubbed with pumice, they jumped, jiggled and twisted. Whipped up by wine, spurred on by alcohol, they whinnied and shied, or collapsed, floppy and dead-beat, on to sofas.

Sometimes, at the end of the evening towards three o'clock in the morning, while all the women were asking men to tell them the time and continally numbing them with the eternal refrain: 'Will you buy me a drink?' a man would come in and say to one of the girls, 'Go and get dressed, I'm taking you home', and he would sit down, his legs crossed, smoking his cigar, waiting until his purchase was handed over to him, packed up in black material. Then you'd hear shouts in the stairwell, the woman asking Madame for a nightdress and fixing her skirts with pins the others had lent her; finally she would come down, scrubbed of her rouge and her powder, and she would go and kiss her friends as if, parting for the night on an adventure, she feared she would never see them again. As they were leaving, the brothel-keeper, leaning against the banisters, would shout in her curt voice: 'I'll expect you tomorrow at midday, don't mess about on the way.'

This was a new fascination for Marthe, this was the attraction of the abyss over which one is leaning, that of a life lived at white-heat, with its somersaults and its pirouettes, the glasses emptied while lying on one's back, the arguments between one girl and another over a ribbon or over a man, and the reconciliations conducted between dashes up and down stairs; she remembered with a singular pleasure those feverish passions that caused her to writhe so deliriously, like the vertiginous frenzy that makes dervishes howl and leap into the air, maddened by the spinning of their wheels.

Besides, this continual state of disorder put all melancholy thoughts to flight, it was a deliberate abdication of day-to-day struggles: the brothel removed all the difficulties of existence, you had nothing to worry about except earning enough to

lose at cards and to get drunk if the customers refused
to pay their share. And yet all the same, how miserable and how abject it all was! No doubt she was
made for the contemptuous kisses of men, but in
those early days how the taste of that filth had stuck
in her throat. The punter would wake up in the
morning, sober, and realising where he'd slept be
furious with himself and full of disgust for the
woman who'd caressed him; he would dress in the
wink of an eye, shaking off the face-powder that
marbled his clothes and leave without even saying
goodbye; she would hear his hurried step on the
stairs, then he'd stop at the door, waiting for a bus to
pass in order to jump in to the street and flee. And
how humiliating it was, whenever she herself spent
the night outside, returning early the next day; the
milkman and the butcher, smoking their pipes on the
steps of their shops, would laugh insultingly and spit
at her feet in revenge for having come and kissed her
the night before!

Finally, thanks to Ginginet, who had vouched for
her saying that he was going to marry her, she was no
longer subject to the attentions of the vice squad,
but the thought that she was once again going to
belong to that herd of women which the police have
to continually stalk and spy on sent a shiver down
her back.

She couldn't hide from herself how distressing she
found the carnal pleasures of this servitude, and yet
she was attracted to them like a moth to the flame of
a lamp; to her, anything – a perilous storm at sea,
being hunted without mercy – seemed preferable to

that heartbreaking loneliness that was eating away
at her.

She would awake from these visions of the past, her
mind in disarray, her cheeks running with sweat, she
would feel as if she were suffocating in her room,
sometimes she would go downstairs to get some air
and trail along the walls with the gait and the ges-
tures of a dying woman. Bright sunlight and the
freshness of the morning would chase away these
dreams, she would collapse onto a bench in some public garden or square, staring at the ground, which she
dug at with the toe of her boots, sieving the dusty
earth through her fingers. But all those children
making mud-pies with their tin buckets exasperated
her; they reminded her of a time when she too wallowed in the dust and planted twigs from a tree amid
a mass of pebbles. She took to wandering around
Paris, and one day when she was ambling along, at a
bend in the road, she chanced upon a barracks at the
hour when beggars come to look for soup.

She stopped in a sort of cul-de-sac, flanked to the
north by the barracks and a few bars where, in the
shade of some boxed pine-trees, old men with bellies like beer-barrels were drinking, and to the south
by stalls selling chips and crêpes, a disreputable-
looking restaurant with its bowls of rice pudding
and blancmange, and a dirty junk-shop at the door
of which hung dresses whose crinoline flesh had
rotted away and whose wire carcasses tinkled in the
wind.

And closer still, at the entrance to the impasse,

three trees with flaccid trunks poked damp and gnarled branches from their cuffs of earth.

A shovelful of wretches had been thrown in the gutter at the foot of these three trees. Here, were poor women with flat chests and complexions of clay, a pile of the bandy-legged and the one-eyed, and a litter of brats who snivelled incredible streams of snot from their noses and sucked their thumbs, waiting for the hour they got their bread.

Leaning, squatting, lying one against the other, they brandished the most unexpected receptacles: casserole pans without handles, stoneware pots tied up with string, dented water-cans, battered mess-tins, broken billy-cans and flower-pots with the bottoms stopped up.

A soldier motioned to them and they all rushed forward, heads down, barking like guard-dogs, then, when their bowls were full, they hurried away with a ravenous look and, backsides on the pavement, feet in the gutter, they greedily gulped down their food.

Marthe shuddered at the sight of one old man who was drinking his soup out of a bedpan, and, totally taken aback, she stared at this face with its matted grey beard, those blinking, bleary eyes, and that nose which, streaked with crimson, pierced the deathly flabby skin of his cheeks. That mangy skull, those rags tied together with thread, the clothes the colour of cow-dung, those moth-eaten breeches, riddled with holes and caked with mud, that waistcoat shrivelled, shrunken and eaten away by constant sun and rain, those unrecognisable shoes, down-at-heel and shapeless, skylights of red leather opening to reveal a big toe; and above all that face, ravaged by every kind of excess, the hideous trembling of his limbs, the hands that were dancing around without him even being aware they were moving, gave the man a look of pitiful poignancy, and she blushed when the beggar came up to her and said in a low voice: 'Don't you recognize me? It's Ginginet.'

'Oh!' she said, taken aback, 'why . . . it's you! Have you really come to this?'

'It was bound to happen; I ate everything, I drank everything, I went bust like a real tradesman; cleaned out, my dear. And what's more, my voice has gone, I can't even hold a note any more, the clapper of the old bell's gone; I must have swallowed it accidentally when I was knocking back a pint. I've changed a bit wouldn't you say, eh? Ah yes, my clothes have neither style nor class, my tweed jacket's out of shape, my trousers are going to pieces and my boots are rotting. But what do you expect? It makes a man old to be poor and to be always thirsty! But come on, talk a bit about yourself. You're still pretty, you know, and, what's more, stunningly well turned out. You must be rich! Oh, well then, you should really loan me a few *sous* for a pint.' And stretching out a filthy sleeve, he added with a hideous smile: 'Spare a copper, princess, it'll bring you good luck.'

There was a sudden flash of rapture in Marthe's eyes: 'Ah!' she said, 'you haven't had much luck since those days when you used to beat me up; it must be hard asking me for a handout, eh?'

Then, at the sight of that face, tanned as if it had been smoked by poverty, her mood changed and pity returned to her heart, she kissed the actor's hideous beard and, giving him all the money she had in her pocket, she said: 'Oh, we're both as bad as each other! All the same, my dear, if we could live our lives over again, you know it would have been better to sweat and slave in an honest job, it would have paid better!'

CHAPTER XII

The man at the Lariboisière Hospital whose job it was not only to help with the book-keeping but to sweep out the autopsy room, pushed open the little door between it and the mortuary, drew the white curtains round the beds, dusted the altar, replenished the chlorine in the pots, pinned back on a coffin a permit that was coming loose, covered a woman's foot with a sheet, took a swig of wine, and without seeming unsettled by the appalling sickly smell which filled both rooms, he went back into the first, which he started mopping out with huge bucketfuls of water.

This room was furnished solely with zinc-topped trestle tables and a fountain that burbled away next to the door. As he passed by, the man cast a casual glance over the corpse of an old man stretched out on the block, legs together, belly swollen like a balloon, face horribly contorted, and, taking a sponge, he set about scrubbing the dissecting tables.

He made sure that the draining hole in each table wasn't blocked, that the tin buckets were correctly hung underneath each opening, then he put his dripping sponge in the basin of the fountain, drank another swig of wine and noticed a large red streak staining the drainage channel; gripped by a sudden mania for tidiness, he ranged along the wall a tub full of sawdust, a pair of rubber boots, and two jars in which some horrible pink-veined mess marinaded in alcohol, then drew the cords of the fanlights which surmounted the two windows. As he went out he found himself in front of two interns, wearing white aprons and black skull-caps, who were just closing the door of the St. Ferdinand ward.

'All the same,' one of them was saying, 'when they brought in poor Ginginet on a stretcher I felt a jolt in my stomach, I relived the whole of my former life in an instant; I remembered the times when, dressed in a red jacket, I'd call out from up in the gods at the Bobino, booing Ginginet and cheering Marthe; I remembered, too, that infamous evening when I took Léo to the Rue de Lourcine.'

'By the way,' said the other, 'whatever happened to your friend Léo?'

'Ah, my dear chap, that's quite a story! He's finally decided to reply to my letter. You can imagine what ... but no, look, you'd better read his letter yourself, it's very interesting, I promise you.'

It was at this moment that the attendant joined them.

'Well, if it isn't old What's-his-name,' they said, 'so what's new?'

'I was just looking for you,' coughed the old man. 'There's an interesting case this morning, it seems. They're going to cut up a man who did himself to death from too much boozing; he had, so the doctor said, a whole heap of diseases each more striking than the last. But you must have heard them speaking about him, Monsieur Charles, he was No. 28 in the St. Vincent ward.'

'Oh, damn,' cried the young man, 'so it's Ginginet

who's died – and here's me wanting to go and ask him
how he was. Well, we'll at least go and see the poor
old devil's autopsy!' And they hurriedly marched off.

The autopsy hadn't yet started, so after
exchanging handshakes with the others there, they
settled themselves next to the water fountain, and,
unfolding Léo's letter, they read in an undertone:

'*You ask me what I'm doing and how I spend my
time? I wander along the river side, my friend, I watch
the water flow past, but I don't fish! – I walk and I sleep
– I also water the flowers, I smoke a big old black pipe, I
drink rough wines and I eat tasty stews, in other words
I'm as fit as a fiddle and I've had a hard job finding an
inkpot in order to write you these few lines.*

'*But let's talk a bit about those I left behind, nearly
two months since, in Paris. Marthe, you tell me, has
gone back to the bawdy-house where she used to live. Ah,
when you were telling me that piece of news you could
have saved yourself all that beating around the bush: it
was finished between us, and you knew it. Forget affection, I'm just not interested in her any more; her life
isn't going to change much now. Admittedly she'll be
better off at some times than at others, but that's about
it; she'll die in a fit of drunkenness or throw herself in
to the Seine on one of her lucid days. Honestly, it's not
worth our while bothering about her, and besides, what
business is it of mine what becomes of her because I've
got a great piece of news to tell you: I'm getting married.*

'*Now, don't you start! Listen: when we used to meet
at my place, we made a lot of jokes and had a lot of
laughs on the subject of marriage. How boring it was,
how stupid it was. Two people come together, at a set*

126

time, to the sound of an organ and in the presence of guests impatient to go and stuff themselves with food that hasn't cost them a thing; then, barring accidents, after a specified number of months, they bring into the world an appalling infant who screams the entire night away under the pretext of suffering from toothache, and so, amid the puffing of pipes, we ordained that an artist should never seriously get entangled with a woman.

'How you used to make me yawn with your talk of Liberty strangled by marriage . . . but then no sooner had you left my place than you'd run off and waste it on the first woman you could pick up! And come to that, didn't you despise those tarts you said you were so taken by, just as much as I did? Wasn't it true that when we found ourselves alone with them, all our instincts as well-educated gentlemen were repulsed by their native vulgarity? Aren't you going to end up just like me, content to marry, as so many of us do, the daughter of some fortune-teller or concierge, who'll spend her time telling cards and never use a comb the day after she's dragged her skirts over the parquet floor of the registry office? And luckier still are those friends with wives whose ragged petticoats are held together with pins and whose mops of hair are all over the place! At least they're usually content to stay at home. But when you do as our friend Brice did, when you marry some bohemian tart, God knows where it'll end! Some big lump of a lass who conceals the graces of a washerwoman beneath her gaudy dresses and puts on the airs of a lady, imposing herself in people's houses even when she hasn't been invited, forcing them to let her sit down at the table she should be serving on . . . that's simply odious, because

127

women like that have a stream of filth gurgling in their mouths which they let loose at dessert, at the same time as they loosen their corsets.

'So there you are, that's where we end up, us others, the free-spirited! Marry your mistress? That's as stupid as Simple Simon, who from fear of the rain jumped into a river! And besides, you still have to find the right mistress. I've had a few, by God; women by the glassful – but all I got was corked wine! It was after that I started running after working lasses, the kind you find hanging on a working man's arm of a Sunday, but they didn't like me. I wasn't from their world, they thought me a poseur, boring in a word, and yet one of them fell for me for a week or so. It was too much, my friend, I had to go out with her – and her hatless – endure her hoots of laughter in the street, and put up with those abominable expressions: "Reely", "For sure", "Ooh, I say!".

'Well, it was in the wake of walks like these that I came to search among the most exotically made-up tarts, looking to awaken desire with a smell of powder, with a touch of make-up, to exult in front of a bosom smothered in a mist of lace that a flash of pale ribbon would disperse. And I was absolutely sincere! I loved a woman less for herself than for her frills and chiffons. How ridiculous! And now that I've come to my senses, I'm amazed at having been so stupid. I won't add to your astonishment by singing my wife's praises; have no fear, I'm not going to tell you that she's beautiful, that she's got eyes like sapphire or jet, or that her lips are crimson. No, she isn't even pretty, but what's that to me? It'll be tedious enough watching her in the evenings mending my socks and being deafened by the cries of my *brats, I agree; but since, in spite of all our theories, we haven't been able to find anything better, I'll content myself with this life, however commonplace it may seem to you.*

'What more can I say? I'm no Clovis, but I've burnt all my old idols; and as for Marthe, since you mention her again at the end of your letter, I forgive her all her vileness, all her treachery; whores like her have this much good about them: they make us love those who resemble them least; they serve as a foil to decency. But I'm boring you, eh, my old friend? Forgive all this non-sense and hold out your hand so I can shake it.'

'Well, I'll be damned . . .!' said the young man, folding up the letter.

But his friends nudged him with their elbows to keep him quiet, and old Briquet, slicing, with a single stroke of the scalpel, through the cranium of the actor, began in his plodding voice:

'Now Messieurs, alcoholism . . .'

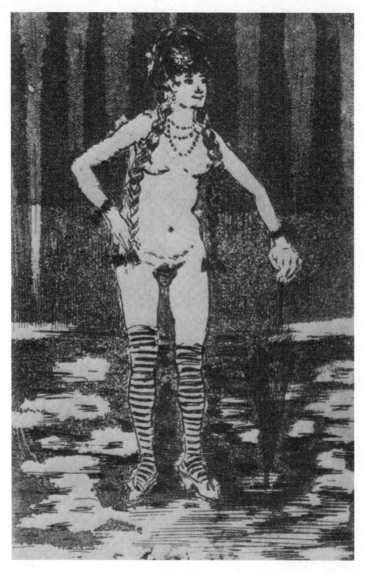

Plate II: This engraving by Jean-Louis Forain was originally
intended as the frontispiece for the French edition of 1879, but
was rejected on the grounds it was too explicit.

NOTES

AUTHOR'S PREFACE

p27 . . . *in the course of overseeing the printing of Marthe.*
Huysmans is not altogether truthful in his account of
Marthe's publishing history. He was actually in Paris not
Brussels when he found out about Goncourt's forthcom-
ing novel, and he hurriedly arranged to extend his leave
of absence from work in order to find a publisher. He left
for Brussels in early August 1876, and once there, he
sought out Camille Lemonnier, a writer whose acquaintance he had made through their contributions to *Le
Musée des Deux-Mondes*. Lemonnier suggested the names
of Callewaert as printer and Jean Gay as publisher and by
12 September he had the printed proofs of the book in his
hands. The dates and places of the novel's composition
that Huysmans appends to the Jean Gay edition of the
book – 'Paris November 1875 to Brussels August 1876' –
are also open to some doubt. On the manuscript used by
the printer the 1875 date has been crossed out and
replaced with 'January 1876', but why this wasn't carried
through into the finished book isn't clear. Perhaps the
answer lies in the strange fact that although Huysmans
says he had finished his book when he found out about
Goncourt's novel, he puts 'Brussels' rather than Paris as
the place where it was finished. This opens the possibility
that he actually hadn't even finished the novel when he
learned about the Goncourt project and that he hurriedly
completed it while he was in Brussels searching for a publisher. This might go some way to explaining the brevity
of the book and its somewhat hastly conclusion, and why

he resorts to the clichéd device of Léo's letter in order to tie up the loose ends of the narrative. As a consequence, Huysmans might have decided to keep the erroneous November 1875 date in order to give the book a longer and more credible gestation period.

p27 . . . *was sold out in a few days.* Huysmans is probably massaging the truth here too. The print run of the Jean Gay edition was unlikely to have been large, given that Huysmans himself was having to pay for the printing. His first book, *Le Drageoir à épices*, which he also had to pay the printing costs for, was published in an edition of only 300 copies. Huysmans tried to smuggle 400 copies of *Marthe* into France on his way back from Brussels, but the majority were confiscated by French customs, and a few years later Henry Kistemaeckers, the infamous Belgian publisher, recalled coming across 350 unsold copies at the printers and selling them to Gay, who then sold them as bibliographical rarities at inflated prices. As Gustave Van Welkenhuyzen in *J.-K. Huysmans et la Belgique* (Paris: Mercure de France, 1935) notes, 'La publication de *Marthe* passe presque inaperçu en Belgique.' ('The publication of *Marthe* passed almost completely unnoticed in Belgium . . .').

p28 . . . *the subject matter I have treated here.* Both Huysmans' and Jean Gay, his publisher, were aware of the risks involved in publishing *Marthe*, and the real possibility of arrest or prosecution that they faced. In order to minimise this risk and to emphasise the book's moral message, Gay included a short Preface which was comprised of a line extracted from the last chapter of the novel: 'Whores like her have this much good about them: they make us love those who resemble them least; they serve as a foil to decency'. Although conditions had changed somewhat by the time Huysmans brought out a French edition of the book in 1879, he was still careful not to go too far and Forain's original engraving for the frontispiece (see Plate II) was rejected as being too risqué and a milder one substituted (see Plate I).

CHAPTER I

p29 . . . *Ginginet.* This unusual name stems from the slang word 'ginginer' (to ogle), and serves to denote his sexually predatory character. It is also possible his name is a pun on 'guinguette' (see note below).

p29 . . . *tonneau.* 'Tonneau', also called the 'the frog game', is a game the aim of which is to throw metal counters into holes, the highest-scoring of which has a cast iron frog with a gaping mouth mounted on the top. The game was popular in the open-air cafés ('guinguettes') with their dance-floors and live music, that flourished on the borders of Paris (in order to avoid the tax on wine imposed within the city boundary) during the nineteenth century. These cafés, which facilitated the free mixing of men and women in the relative anonymity of the crowd, had a reputation among the middle classes as places of loose and immoral behaviour.

p30 . . . *an old rebeck.* A medieval stringed instrument that was played with a bow.

p30 . . . *a wheezing flageolet.* A wind instrument with a wedge-shaped mouthpiece like the recorder, the flageolet was a common instrument in French orchestras in the nineteeth century.

p31 . . . *Bobino theatre.* A theatre situated at the junction of the Rue Madame and the Rue de Fleurus, near the Jardin du Luxembourg, which Huysmans used to frequent in the 1860s. It was with an article on one of the revues playing at the Bobino that Huysmans made his journalistic debut. See note for *Monthly Review* below.

p32 . . . *drumming from the stalls.* In the original Huysmans uses the words 'Larifla, fla fla', a reference to a military march or air probably made popular around the time of Napoléon, with the repetition of 'fla, fla' being an onomatopoeic device that recalls the sound of drums in battle.

p34 . . . *The Monthly Review.* Huysmans' first pieces of journalism were published in *La Revue Mensuelle* (*The Monthly Review*). The first, on contemporary landscape artists, was published on 25 November 1867, and the second, published the following month, was a brief piece of dramatic criticism, a review of a show called *La Vogue Parisienne.* In it, Huysmans seemed to praise almost every member of the cast. Following a tip from Robert Baldick in the early 1950s, Pierre Lambert found the name and address of the publisher of the journal, Monsieur Le Hire, and from this went on to discover the two long-lost reviews. They were published for the first time in book form in a critical edition of *Marthe* edited by Pierre Cogny (Paris: Le Cercle du Livre, 1955).

p35 . . . *at Amboise when I was lead tenor at the Grand Theatre.* The Grand Theatre at Amboise in the Loire is an impressive provincial theatre, designed by architect Léon Rohard and built between 1868–1872.

CHAPTER II

p37 . . . *worker in artificial pearls.* As part of his research for the novel Huysmans was taken to an artificial pearl factory by his friend Ludovic de Francmesnil, but it is also possible that he got some of his information about the artifical pearl-making process from *Diamants et Pierres Précieuses* written by Louis Dieulafait, professor of Geology and Mineralogy at the Faculty of Sciences in Marseilles, and published in 1874.

p38 . . . *'pure septembral juice'*. The archaic phrase 'purée septembrale' has its literary origins in Rabelais' *Gargantua and Pantagruel*, but it was also used by Balzac in *Lost Illusions*.

p38 . . . *orient*. A technical term used to describe the unique play of colours on the surface of a real pearl and which gives it its distinctive character. The 'orient' of a genuine pearl is almost impossible to replicate by artificial means.

p41 . . . *torments of Tantalus*. Tantalus, the son of the god Zeus and Pluto (the daughter of Cronos the Titan), was a legendary king of Sipylus who was supposed to have stolen food from the gods and given it to mortals. As a punishment, Tantalus was condemned to spend an eternity in Hades, both hungry and thirsty. He had to stand in water up to his chin, but when he tried to drink the water drained away, and though boughs of fruit dangled above his head, when he tried to reach for them the wind would blow them away.

p41 . . . *sword of Brennus*. When the leader of the Gauls, Brennus, defeated the Romans in 390 BC, he agreed to withdraw his army for a payment of a thousand pounds in gold. According to Livy, when the Romans complained that the weights the Gauls were using were too heavy, a Gaul soldier threw his sword into the balance and uttered the words '*Vae Victis!*' (Woe to the vanquished).

p42 . . . *drifted along with the flow*. 'A vau-l'eau' in the original. Huysmans would later use this phrase as the title for a short novel published in 1882. This metaphor of being carried along inexorably by the tide of events frequently recurs in Huysmans' work.

p44 . . . *a few months pregnant.* According to Robert Baldick, this incident is based on Huysmans' own experience, see *The Life of J.-K. Huysmans*, Chapter 2 (Dedalus, 2006).

CHAPTER III

p48 . . . *frills of her dressing-gown.* Huysmans uses 'fanfioles' in the original, an obscure word probably formed by the conjunction of 'fanfreluche' (frills and furbelows) and 'babiole' (trifle or knick-knack). The idea that feminine dress and adornment is a stimulant to sexual desire recurs throughout Huysmans' early work. Edmond and Jules de Goncourt also used the word 'fanfioles' in their description of Madame de Pompadour in *L'Art du XVIIIe siècle.*

p51 . . . *indefinable anguish seized her by the throat.* A woman suspected of being a prostitute could be stopped by the police and forced to submit to a physical examination. Once registered by the police as a prostitute, she would have to go for regular medical check-ups to ensure she hadn't contracted a venereal disease. Also see note in Chapter V for *anti-venereal dispensary.*

p52 . . . *Mengin crayons.* Mengin (sometimes incorrectly spelled Mangin) was a well-known crayon manufacturer, based in the Rue de Faubourg Saint Martin in Paris. Mengin made his name by the extravagant way in which he hawked and sold his crayons, giving demonstrations of his wares in the street while distinctively dressed as a

Plate III: *The Bean King* by Jacob Jordaens (1593–1678).

Plate IV: *The Rake's Progress (Plate III)* by William Hogarth (1697–1764).

Spanish conquistador, complete with crested helmet. He died in 1864.

CHAPTER IV

p56 . . . *Jordaens' The Bean King*. Jacob Jordaens (1593–1678) painted several versions of this picture, but the one Huysmans describes is probably the one now at the Royal Museum of Fine Arts in Brussels (see Plate III). The picture describes the traditional festivities surrounding 'Twelfth Night', in which a cake is served containing a single bean. The guest who finds the bean becomes the king of the feast, he gets to wear a crown, nominate his queen and appoint the other guests as his court. The highlight of the evening is when the 'king' takes his first drink, at which the rest of the company shouts 'The King drinks!' and the meal begins.

p57 . . . *A Harlot's Progress*. The picture Huysmans actually describes is not from Hogarth's *A Harlot's Progress* (1732), but from a later series, *A Rake's Progress* (1735). Although the two series depict a similar set of vices and follies, Huysmans' mistake is revealing, as it wrongly implies that the young man in the picture, Tom Rakewell, is the prostitute's victim, rather than being the author of his own moral downfall (see Plate IV).

p59 . . . *with succubi or phantoms like those in Goya's pictures*. Interestingly, the phantoms haunting Léo's imagination prefigure those of Jacques Marles in *En Rade* and Durtal in *Là-bas*.

p60 . . . *Cythera*. In mythology, the island of Cythera (Kythira) was the birthplace of Venus, the goddess of love. A subsequent myth associated with this idea, in which a man would go to Cythera and meet his true female counterpart with whom he would experience a day of bliss before returning to the real world, took hold in French culture during the eighteenth century and was most notably depicted in Antoine Watteau's *Embarkation for Cythera*. References to the Cythera myth can also be found in the work of a number of nineteenth-century poets, such as Charles Baudelaire and Gerard de Nerval.

p62 . . . *thinking of the exploits of Hercules.* The reference to Hercules seems a little ambiguous. The goddess Hera, jealous of Jupiter's infidelity, tricked Hercules into killing his wife and child. It was in an attempt to expiate this crime, and to gain his immortality, that Hercules performed his twelve labours.

p64 . . . *little sprite cutting a caper on top of his column.* The gilded statue on top of the bronze column in the Place de la Bastille is a winged personification of the spirit of Liberty. The column itself was erected by the French government between 1833 and 1840 to honour the victims of the 'Trois Glorieuses', the three glorious days of the revolution.

CHAPTER V

p68 . . . *Meanwhile his money galloped away.* Huysmans borrowed this image from a line in a poem by Joachim du Bellay (1522–1560) called *La Complainte du désespéré*.

p77 . . . *anti-venereal dispensary.* The *contrôle sanitaire*, or health check, was a requirement for all registered prostitutes. Prostitutes who lived and worked in a brothel were checked on the premises, whereas those who worked independently were examined at the city dispensary. In Paris, the *dispensaire antivénérien* was in the courtyard of the prefecture of police.

p77 . . . *Titine*. Often used in the literature of the time to denote a girl of easy virtue or suspect moral character.

p78 . . . *statue of the King*. The equestrian statue of Henri IV on the Pont Neuf, which he opened in 1607. The original statue was torn down during the French Revolution, but a replacement from the original mould was recast in 1818 using bronze from a statue of Napoléon formerly in the Place Vendôme.

p79 . . . *Lisette*. A stock name in the theatre for the figure of the *soubrette* or the light-hearted working girl.

p79 . . . *come and down a glass of brandy*. In the original, Huysmans uses the word 'pitancher', thieves' slang for a drink, which he may either have come across during the course of his work at the Sûreté Générale, the French security service, to which he had been moved at the start of 1876, or read in Eugène Sue's *The Mysteries of Paris*.

CHAPTER VI

p83 . . . *address yourself to the Prefecture of Police*. The workings of the Prefecture of Police would have been familiar to Huysmans, as it was overseen by the Ministry of the Interior where he himself worked.

CHAPTER VII

p88 . . . *Eau de Botot*. Invented in 1755 by Dr Julien Botot and approved by the Académie de Médecine, Eau de Botot was a herbal mouthwash widely used during the nineteenth century. Jules Cheret produced an advertising poster for it.

p88 . . . *Chypre perfume*. 'Chypre' is the French name for Cyprus, the birthplace of the goddess of love, Venus. It is probable that Huysmans took the name from a real perfume, though larger perfume manufacturers such as Guerlain and François Coty didn't market their own Chypre perfume until 1909 and 1917 respectively.

p90 . . . *one of his friends, an intern at the Lariboisière Hospital.* This is probably a thinly disguised portrait of Huysmans' friend Henry Céard (1851–1924), a fellow writer in the Médan circle. Céard began his career studying medicine under Dr Léon Beaufort, a surgeon at the Lariboisière, but he abandoned his studies in 1872 and the following year he entered the Ministry of War. See also note in Chapter XII for *Lariboisière Hospital.*

CHAPTER VIII

p91 . . . *Rue de Lourcine.* The name of the Rue de Lourcine was changed in 1890, and now comprises three separate streets: Rue Broca, Rue Edouard Quénu, and Rue Léon-Maurice Nordmann.

p91 . . . *aniseed-flavoured Géromé cheese decomposed.* A similar detail was used in Chapter 5 of Zola's *Le Ventre de Paris* (1873): 'Et, derrière les balances, dans sa boîte mince, un géromé anisé répandait une infection telle, que des mouches étaient tombées autour de la boîte, sur le marbre rouge veiné de gris.' (And in a fragile box behind the scales, an aniseed-flavoured Géromé diffused such a pestilential smell that dead flies had fallen all around the box onto the red, grey-veined marble slab.')

p94 . . . *Mam'selle Sidonie.* Huysmans was fascinated by the artifice of femininity, especially in relation to clothes and make-up. In the pantomime he wrote and published with Léon Hennique, *Pierrot sceptique* (1881), Pierrot falls in love with a hairdresser's dummy, La Sidonie.

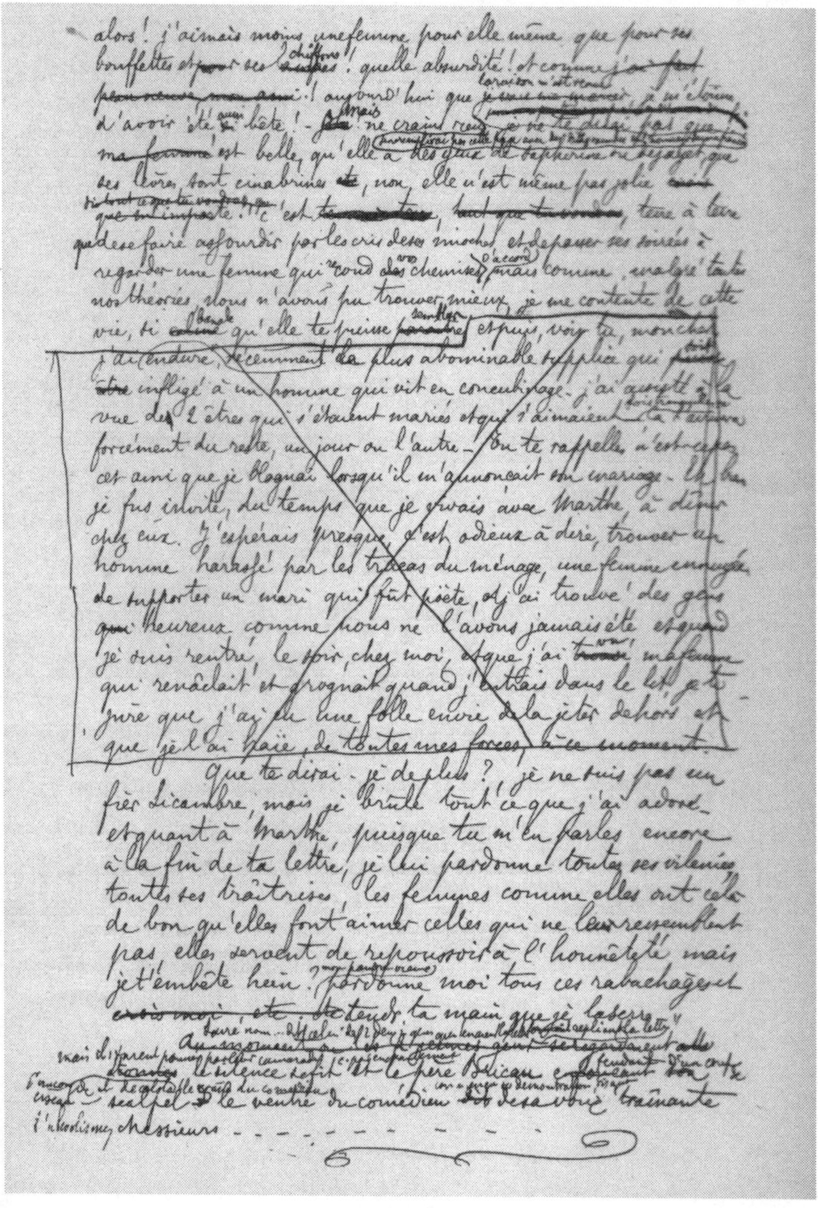

Plate V: The final page of the original manuscript of *Marthe,
histoire d'une fille.*

p94 . . . *knees in the air*. The phrase Huysmans uses in the original, 'à jambes rebindaines', is another Rabelaisian phrase, from Book Two, Chapter 29 of *Gargantua and Pantagruel*: 'Pantagruel . . . le frappa d'un si grand coup de pied au ventre, qu'il le jeta en arrière à jambes rebindaines' (Pantagruel struck him such a blow with his foot against the belly, that he made him fall backwards, head over heels).

p95 . . . *Can-can! Let's do the can-can!* In the original, Huysmans uses the word 'chahut', the name of an eccentric and slightly deranged dance, a little like the can-can, which was characterised by improvised and risqué steps, and accompanied by shouts and whoops. It was often performed at open-air café-concerts or 'guinguettes'.

p97 . . . *Bischof*. A wine from Bordeaux which was an aromatic mix of bitter orange ('bigarade'), sugar and spices ('muscade' and 'cannelle'). Its name, the German for 'bishop', was inspired by its purple colour.

CHAPTER IX

p102 . . . *Cassian purple*. The discovery of Cassian purple, used for colouring glass and ceramics, is attributed to Andreas Cassius, a German physician of the seventeenth century. However, the pigment was actually in use for a number of years before Cassius wrote about it. Huysmans often employed technical names of paints and colours used by artists in his work, as if emphasising both his artistic ancestry and his artistic credentials.

CHAPTER X

p106 . . . *opoponax*. A gum resin with an exotic scent, similar to myrrh, used in perfumes. Huysmans makes a number of references to it in his work, including 'Similitudes', which was written in 1876 and published in *Parisian Sketches* (1880). In the preface he wrote to a book of Théodore Hannon's poems, *Rimes de Joie* (1881), Huysmans described the poem 'Opoponax' as the most original in the collection.

p113 . . . *a kind of harbour.* The notion that human beings periodically need to shelter from the storms of life is expressed through another maritime metaphor that recurs throughout Huysmans' work. The title of his 1887 novel *En Rade*, for example, literally means 'in dry dock' or 'at harbour'.

CHAPTER XI

p115 . . . *stigmata of infamy, the kiss-curl.* According to Gustave Geffroy, an art critic who got to know Huysmans quite well in his later years, the kiss-curl was frequently sported by pimps during this period.

CHAPTER XII

p124 . . . *Lariboisière Hospital.* Huysmans was taken to the Lariboisière Hospital to witness an autopsy by Henry Céard who, though no longer studying at the hospital, still had contacts there. Afterwards, wanting his friend to check the accuracy of his descriptions, Huysmans wrote to Céard inviting him to 'come and eat a cutlet with me, and see if my hospital is all right'.

p129 . . . *however commonplace it may seem to you.* The original handwritten manuscript of *Marthe* includes the following paragraph (see Plate V), which Huysmans decided to delete before publication: '. . . you see, my friend, I recently endured the most abominable torment that can be inflicted on a man who lives with his mistress. I witnessed the sight of two people who got married and who love each other, which happens every now and then. You remember the friend I made jokes about when he announced he was getting married? Well, I was invited to dinner with him while I was still living with Marthe. I was hoping to find, though it's terrible to admit it, a man harassed by household cares, and a woman fed up with having to support a poet for a husband. And yet I found two people happier than we've ever been, and after I returned home that evening and looked at the woman who grunted and groaned when I got into bed, I swear to you that I had a mad desire to throw her out, and that at that moment I hated her with all my being.'

p129 . . . *Clovis*. Clovis, King of the Francs, converted to Christianity and was baptised on Christmas day 496. As he was immersing Clovis in the baptismal waters, bishop Rémy said to him: 'Bow your head, proud Sicambrian, humbly bow. Worship that which you used to burn, and burn that which you used to worship.'

p129 . . . *Now messieurs, alcoholism*. Huysmans' novel ends with a suitably Naturalistic flourish. The autopsy table recalls Zola's famous self-defence of the modern writer in his preface-cum-manifesto to *Thèrese Raquin* (1869) that he was 'simply applying to two living bodies the analytical method that surgeons apply to corpses'.

Recommended Reading

If you have enjoyed reading *Marthe* and would like to read another book by J.-K. Huysmans we have published another five:

Là-Bas
En Route
The Cathedral
The Oblate of St Benedict
Parisian Sketches

We have also published a biography of J.-K.Huysmans:

The Life of J.-K. Huysmans – Robert Baldick

There are other books on our list which should appeal to you if you like the books of J.-K. Huysmans :

Paris Noir – Jacques Yonnet
Le Calvaire –Octave Mirbeau
Abbé Jules – Octave Mirbeau
Sebastian Roch –Octave Mirbeau
Torture Garden – Octave Mirbeau
The Diary of a Chambermaid –Octave Mirbeau
Monsieur de Phocas – Jean Lorrain
The Golem – Gustav Meyrink
The Maimed –Hermann Ungar
The Class –Hermann Ungar

These can be bought from you local bookshop or online from amazon.co.uk or amazon.com or direct from Dedalus. Please write to **Cash Sales, Dedalus Limited, Langford Lodge, St Judith's Lane, Sawtry, Cambs, PE28 5XE**. For further details of the Dedalus list please go to our website www.dedalusbooks.com or write to us for a catalogue.

Là-Bas – J.-K. Huysmans

'The protagonist, Durtal, is investigating the life of Gilles de Rais, mass-murderer and unlikely companion-in-arms of Joan of Arc. Long meditation on the nature of art, guilt, the satanic and the divine take him to a black mass. This superb new translation by Brendan King vividly recalls the allusive, proto-expressionist vigour of the original; images snarl and spring at the reader.'

Murrough O'Brien in The Independent on Sunday

'As with most of Huysmans' books, the pleasure in reading is not necessarily from its overarching plot-line, but in set pieces, such as the extraordinary sequences in which Gilles de Rais wanders through a wood that suddenly metamorphoses into a series of copulating organic forms, the justly famous word-painting of Matthias Grunewald's Crucifixion altar-piece, or the brutally erotic scenes, crackling with sexual tension, between Durtal and Madame Chantelouve. If it is about any-thing, *Là-Bas* is about Good and Evil. This enlightening new translation will be especially useful to students of literature.'

Beryl Bainbridge in The Spectator

'The classic tale of satanism and sexual obsession in nineteenth-century Paris, in an attractive new edition. Strong meat for diseased imaginations.'

Time Out

'Sex, satanism and alchemy are the themes of this cult curio, which understandably caused shock waves in the Parisian literary world when it was first published in 1891. This Gothic shocker is not for the faint-hearted.'

Jerome Boyd Maunsell in The Times

£8.99   **ISBN 1 873982 74 7**   **294p**   **B. Format**

Parisian Sketches – J.-K.Huysmans

'No one, not even Toulouse-Lautrec, was so tireless a tracker of Paris's genius loci as Huysmans. Like many of his radical contemporaries, he was obsessed by the idea of beauty within the ugliness of back-street Paris, by the thought that the distortions of depravity presented a truer picture of our spiritual nature than conventional religion or revolutionary excess. The excellent introduction to these cameos show how Huysmans saw his art as complementary to the painter's.'

Murrough Obrien in The Independent on Sunday

'First published in the 1880s, this collection of atmospheric journalism reveals the great decadent ("nature is only interesting when sick and distressed") moving from a broadly naturalistic, almost Dickensian style; as in a 1879 account of the Folies Bergère; to the heightened subjectivity of "Nightmare", inspired by Odilon Redon: "blurred infusoria, vague flagellates, bizarre protoplasms". Huysmans created evocative prose-pictures of Parisian life; a visit to the barber, a gloomy railway café, a chestnut-seller; that merit comparison with the pictures of Caillebotte, Degas and Atget.'

Christopher Hirst in the Independent

'The nouveau journalism described people who were artists' subjects – a hefty blonde trapeze artist at the Folies Bergère shaking the safety net, a journeyman baker like a powered Pierrot pummelling flaccid dough with mighty blows. And places, too, out on the fetid edges of a capital that was jerry-building distant arrondissements as fast as possible after Haussman had remodelled the ancient rues into grand boulevards. Huysmans was a genuine flaneur – no posing and no lounging, he was up and out every day filling notebooks with info we wouldn't otherwise now know about, such as the varied erotic odours of the female armpit before the invention of antiperspirant.'

VR in the Guardian

£6.99   ISBN 1 903517 24 9   196p   B.Format

The Life of J.-K. Huysmans – **Robert Baldick**

'Dedalus have been steadily printing the novels of the astonishing 19th-century French novelist Joris-Karl Huysmans and
as a bonus have reissued Robert Baldick's classic biography,
one of the most elegant, stimulating and moving of all literary
biographies, right up there with Leon Edel's *James* and
George Painter's *Proust*, revised and annotated by Brendan
King. The life and the work are equally compelling.'
Simon Callow in The Guardian's Summer Reading

'Huysmans was an obsessive smoker and convert to Rome. He
knew everyone – Degas, Verlaine, Zola. He wrote about his
own sins, about God, the Devil, art and women. His mistress
died in an insane asylum and he died of cancer. One could say
his life followed the usual lines.'
Beryl Bainbridge in The Oldie's Summer Reading

'Baldick has produced the authorative biography which
supercedes all previous ones, and which is the soundest, fullest
and most scholarly in any language.'
Enid Starkie in The New Statesman

'An enormous amount of research must have gone into pro-
ducing this excellent book. The trouble was well spent. Not
only is a considerable author displayed in all his many sides,
but also a great fragment of French intellectual life is revealed
in the process.'
Anthony Powell

£15.00   **ISBN 1 903517 43 5   592p   B. Format**

Torture Garden – Octave Mirbeau

'This hideously decadent *fin-de-siècle* novel by the French anarchist Mirbeau has become an underground classic. A cynical first half exposes the rottenness of politics, commerce and the petit bourgeois; in the second half, our totally corrupt narrator travels to China and meets the extraordinary Clara. She shows him the *Torture Garden*, a place of exotic flowers and baroque sadism. There are satirical and allegorical dimensions, but it remains irreducibly horrible.'
>   *Phil Baker in The Sunday Times*

'First published in 1898 this decadent classic flays civilised society down to its hypocritical bones and is *le dernier cri* in kinky exoticism.'
>   *Anne Billson in Time Out*

'The *Torture Garden* by Mirbeau: a quite stunning investigation into the furthest extremities of physical love. Almost post-modern in style and structure, it is genuinely intelligent, and therefore deeply unsettling work.'
>   *Philip Kane in The Independent on Sunday*

'First published in Paris's scandal-soaked *fin-de-siècle* by a French anarchist with a taste for exposing political corruption and a unique slant on sadism, *Torture Garden* has always been a distinctly underground favourite until now. That's unlikely to remain so, not so much because of Mirbeau's political attitudes – which have a stunningly modern staccato brash-ness – but because of his distinctly kinky eroticism. The story takes us from the backstabbing Parisian chattering classes to the hidden pleasures and pains of a Chinese torture garden. Mirbeau asks which of the two societies is really the more civilised, but even modern readers will find themselves reel-ing at the extent to which he clearly loves to wallow in decadence.'
>   *The Scotsman*

£7.99   ISBN 1 873982 53 4   210p   B. Format